Corona

Bushra Rehman

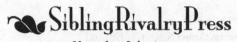

Sibling Rivalry Press

Alexander, Arkansas

www.siblingrivalrypress.com

Sibling Rivalry Press, LLC
13913 Magnolia Glen Drive
Alexander, AR 72002

info@siblingrivalrypress.com
www.siblingrivalrypress.com

ISBN: 978-1-937420-39-0
Library of Congress Control Number: 2013933981
First Sibling Rivalry Press Edition, August 2013

Corona

Corona

Acknowledgements

The stories in this collection have appeared in: *Everything All At Once* (Queens Museum of Art), *And the World Changed: Contemporary Stories by Pakistani Women* (Feminist Press), *Das vermessene Paradies Positionen zu New York* (House of World Cultures), *Pulp Net*, and *Mizna: Prose, Poetry and Art Exploring Arab America*. Excerpts have also appeared in *The New York Times* and *Sepia Mutiny*.

Corona

Contents

Corona
(and I'm not talking about the beer)
Corona, Queens
1983

Corona, and I'm not talking about the beer. I'm talking about a little village perched under the number 7 train in Queens between Junction Boulevard and 111th Street. I'm talking about the Corona Ice King, Spaghetti Park, and P.S. 19. The Corona F. Scott Fitzgerald called the "valley of ashes" as the Great Gatsby drove past it on his night of carousal but what me and my own know as home. And we didn't know about any valley of ashes because by then it had been topped off by our houses. You know, the kind made from brick, this tan color no self-respecting brick would be at all. That's Corona.

And you know that song by Paul Simon, the one where he says, "I'm on my way . . . I don't know where I'm going . . . I'm on my way . . . I'm taking my time, and I don't know where. Good-bye to Rosie, queen of Corona. See you, me, and Julio down by the schoolyard . . ." Well, I used to always tell people it was Corona he was singing about, but I didn't know if it was true because why would Paul Simon be singing about Corona? I mean, I didn't see many white people there unless they were policemen or firemen, and I didn't think Paul Simon had ever been one of those.

Then I saw these old pictures of Simon and Garfunkel, and there they were standing in front of one of those tan brick homes. I couldn't believe it. All this time I was trying to have fake Corona pride, that was real Corona pride. The lie I thought was a lie was actually true.

"Good-bye Rosie, queen of Corona. See you, me, and Julio

down by the school yard, see you, me, and Julio down by the school yard . . ."

I had a Julio, too. We didn't hang out down by the school yard like Paul Simon must have with his Julio. We didn't hang out anywhere at all. But I loved him in the way you only could when you were a child. Julio had beauty marks all over, as if it wasn't obvious to everyone how he looked. He carried his body like fire, matchstick, rope.

All the girls in school showed off for Julio: jumping Double Dutch, cursing and fighting. In Corona, girls learned early to flash skin, flirt, chew gum, and play games to bring the boys down to their knees, even though it would usually end up the other way around. But I was not one of them. My mother didn't let me wear skirts, especially the kind of short skirts the other girls wore with their hairless legs and fearless way of flicking their hips. I watched them flirt with Julio, my back against the brick wall.

Julio was my next-door neighbor and in my same fourth-grade class in school. We walked the same way home. Not together of course. He walked ahead of me with his friends, and they'd be whooping and screaming and pulling roses out whenever we went past this Korean house that had so many roses they grew up and over through the fence like they were some kind of convicts trying to scale the walls.

The Korean grandmother would have to stand in the yard as soon as the school bell rang and wave her stick and scream at all of us so we wouldn't pull out every last one. But Julio always managed to steal a rose. He was quick and thin. All the other boys rallied around him. He could leap almost to the top of the fence, grab a rose, and then fall back on the pack of boys, pushing one of them nearly into the street, partly from the impact and partly for the joy of it. Then he'd shake the hair out of his eyes and laugh.

But one day the Korean grandmother got smart. She wasn't waiting inside the fence yelling like she usually was. She hid behind a car across the street, and when Julio and his friends came around, she was right behind them. She grabbed Julio by one of his skinny arms and pulled him into the garden. "Bad boy! Tell me where you live!" She shook him again. "Tell me where you live!"

Julio's friends stopped. Their hands were still pushed through the gaps in the fence. This was new. They didn't know whether to run away or run in. They stood like statues waiting for someone to do or say something to make things normal again. Julio was the one who did. He pulled back with all his thin weight and said to her face, "I don't need to tell you where I live you smelly ching-chong."

The grandmother stopped shaking him. Her mouth opened, but what she wanted to say, she could not. I felt shame pulse through me, a burning flame. Just then, one of Julio's friends picked up a beer can from the street and threw it. It missed her, but the next thing I knew, there was a howl and a rush. All the boys started picking up litter and glass bottles that had been left on the street and throwing them.

The grandmother's fingers lost their grip, and when she ran into the house, all the boys ran into the garden and started pulling roses off the branches. All of them: the tea lemon, the hot pink, the deep red, the little ones with flecks of gold in their skin. The thorns tore through their fingers, but they didn't let it stop them. It was their first time in the garden, and now it was theirs.

By this time, all the kids who walked home that way, and even some who didn't, had stopped to see what was happening. I stood with my face pressed against the chain links.

Then I saw Julio. He was smiling and his arms were full of tattered roses. He looked like a crown prince as he walked out of the garden and started throwing flowers at the children who were too scared to run in. When he saw me, he stopped. For a second, I could see he couldn't trust me not to tell.

Then he smiled, the first time he had ever really smiled at me. He picked out a rose. It was hot pink, stiff, just beginning to open.

"Here," he said and threw the rose at my feet.

Pioneer Spirit
Salem, Massachusetts
August 1995

My first summer away from Queens I worked in Salem, a city so famous for burning women, its whole economy was based on it. I got a job at a recreated seventeenth-century village called Pioneer Spirit. It was like a run down Plimoth Plantation, the bastard child where all the druggies and misfits went, the ones who couldn't be trusted to stay in character in Plimoth, the ones who would forget.

Pioneer Spirit was different than Plimoth in that we didn't have to act like we were pilgrims. Mostly we just hung out in costume. Once or twice a day each of us gave tours. We had a line-up, and when it was your turn and you heard the bell, you went to the Governor's House to see who had shown up, what poor tourist had been led astray, had come to Salem to see witches and somehow got duped into taking our tour of pre-witch trial Salem: Pioneer Spirit 1630, a living history museum.

Some of the folks who worked there were history buffs. They wore their costumes even when they weren't working and actually read about Salem's history, but most of us, Walter, June, and me, were just folks who couldn't deal with having any kind of real job, stoners who liked the idea of dressing up in costumes from the 1600s. We got by on one history book we rotated among us and our imaginations.

On my first day, they gave me a white bonnet, red jacket, white undershirt, and brown wool skirt. The woman who was training us warned me it was extremely flammable, so I should try not to get too close to the fire when demonstrating how to

18

make Johnny cakes for the tourists. She said it in this way that made me feel she wasn't kidding. That many women had come and gone before me, up in flames.

Johnny cakes were made out of cornmeal and a little sugar. Puritans took them along when they went on journeys, but they couldn't pronounce "journey" right so the cakes were called Johnny cakes. I didn't really know if this was true, but I said it on every tour. I would stand back from the fire, hitch up my skirt (in a very non-Puritan way), and cook those cakes in cast-iron pans which could really have been from the 1600s, they were so old and dirty. I wasn't allowed to let the tourists taste the cakes, but mine always came out so burnt no one ever asked.

At the end of my first week, I got a group made up of seven Harley bikers and one older couple. The bikers were grizzly-bearded and big and made me look like a tiny Puritan doll when I stood next to them. I was terrified, but I pulled myself up to my full five feet and looked them in their faces. If I took away their motorcycles and muscles, they looked just like my beard-ed Muslim uncles in Queens. Somehow my costume had me feeling brave, as if I really was a ghost of the past. If anyone tried to touch me, their hands would just pass through.

That day was pretty hot, and my wool skirt and jacket were itching. I started off the tour by taking the bikers and the older couple to the dugouts. There were seven bikers, all different heights and widths, but they all looked like they had been coated with the same dirt from the open road. Standing next to them, the older couple seemed ironed out, pink, and unbelievably clean.

The village was set up to go chronologically, from how the Puritans lived when they were FOBs to how they "advanced," until they were living just like the English in London, except surrounded by "savages" and wilderness instead of the ash and sin they had left behind. When everyone was gathered around, I began my tour:

"The Puritans got here during a dreadful winter. They had been lost at sea, and when they arrived, the snow was yea high." I put my hand up to my chest. "There were no houses set up with fireplaces and maids, so someone had the brilliant idea to dig homes into the sides of the hills—these dugouts. You can come closer and look in." I waved my arms grandly at the not-so-grand entrance. The old couple pushed ahead of the Harley bikers to take a peek. "Kind of dark and spooky. Not really welcoming. Now imagine fifteen to twenty men, women, and children all cramped in here, stuck, homesick, and really sick too." Whenever I said that part, I realized it sounded like the Pakistani families I knew back in Queens, but no, I had to focus.

"Most of the Puritans died that first winter when they arrived. Of course, the Native Americans probably would have been happy if all of them had died." The bikers chuckled, but the older couple looked shocked. They seemed to get paler, and I made a mental note to never use that joke again on a tour.

"Alrighty then." I moved the group a bit abruptly to the pen next to the dugouts where we kept our historically accurate goats. The couple and the Harley bikers thankfully followed me.

"Well these are our goats. There's Snowball and that's

Rosemary and Thyme. Now these goats are not your average goats. They're historical. Not stuffed, they're real." The goats bleated in affirmation. "But they're pure bred so they look, act, eat, sound, chew, and well, every other goat activity, they do it just like the goats back then."

The lady knelt down by the pen and started luring Rosemary with a blade of grass. "They're pretty big." Rosemary ignored her, nonchalantly turned her head, and bleated. I don't think she appreciated the crack on her weight.

"Yes, please don't get too close. Remember these are not petting goats, and they can get pretty nasty. It's true. They're big because they're pregnant, and they look just like the pregnant Puritan goats from historical times. If you come back in a few weeks, there will be babies." I had been told by Ron, my boss, to promote Pioneer Spirit since it was on the verge of being shut down.

The older man said in a dry voice, "Where's the father?"

"Oh, we'll meet Winthrop, the daddy, in a moment. He's named after the first governor of Massachusetts, but he had to be fenced off in another part of the village for getting a little too frisky, and believe me, Puritan goats get frisky just like the rest." The Harley bikers laughed, which was a relief for me, but the older couple turned pink.

Like Winthrop on the ill-fated ship, the Arabella, I turned and motioned for them to follow me. "We used to have Puritan chickens too, but those, well those, had to be taken away because, you see, Puritan chickens weren't like the scrawny weaklings we eat nowadays. They had wings long enough to fly. Yes, fly. They always ended up on top of the Governor's House. We spent so much time pulling them down, we barely had any time for doing other Puritan things. Like, um . . ." I had to think of what Puritans did. "Like praying."

We came to the bottom of a hill. "Okay then, if you follow me, just up this hill along the stream . . ."

"What stream?" It was the dry, old man again.

"Oh, the stream." Shit. Will the Blacksmith was supposed to turn it on in the morning. "Just one second." I ran up cursing Will and found the water tap in the rocks that was supposed to create the stream. At first I thought it was stuck, but I finally got it to twist. Brown water shot out, and after a few seconds, it was clear. I ran back trying not to trip on my skirt.

"Okay, here's the stream!" They all looked up. Down the rocks, a trickle of water was slowly inching toward us. "It hasn't rained, so it's drying up. But yes, if you follow me . . ."

I could tell the Harley bikers were getting a kick out of my tour. The other couple I could still try to win over. They all had to be impressed by the next part. The Harley bikers were kicking up dust, and the old man and lady were doing everything to dodge the clouds rising into their faces.

"What is that?" The wife pointed to what looked like a giant piece of Shredded Wheat.

I stopped the tour. "This strange looking structure you see is an English Wigwam. Basically, the English got tired of living like cave people in the dugouts. And you know the saying, 'If you live with Romans, act like Romans' or something like that? Well the Puritans didn't really want to act like Native Americans, but they just looked so warm and healthy, and with the Puritans dying off so fast, they knew they would have to do something to adapt, so they copied the wigwam design. But they couldn't give up their Englishness. They missed their thatched roofs so much, they decided to thatch their wigwams instead of using fresh leaves."

I brought them inside where it was cool and dark. "The only problem was these English Wigwams were basically stacks of hay which could burn down in a matter of seconds with nothing more than a spark, and since the inside of the wigwam was used for cooking food like Johnny cakes, many families died, this time not from the cold but from being burned alive."

"Anybody got a light?" It was one of the Harley bikers. I laughed and nicknamed him Chuckles in my head.

I could feel the old man getting wound up right behind me, even though it was dark, and I couldn't see his face. I was getting pretty tired of giving the tour. I couldn't wait to get out of my bonnet and meet up with the rest of the Puritan gang for lunch. We usually got high behind John the Blacksmith's Shop. I decided to skip a few stops.

"Okay, next is Winthrop's house. The governor, not the goat." They laughed, but their laughter sounded more like bleating than anything else.

The Governor's House was two stories with real glass windows. Compared to the rest of the homes, it was a mansion. I guess some things never change.

I brought them into the front room where there was a stuffed turkey and a gun hanging above the fireplace. I waited for everyone to gather around. The old man and woman were lagging behind. They looked like they were disagreeing. He was whispering to her angrily. I tried hard not to look worried. There had already been complaints about our tours. A few minutes later, they joined us, and I was able to breathe.

I continued: "The Puritans were terrible hunters. They

would rush through the forest trampling everything in sight, making a ton of noise, shouting left and right, letting the animals know for miles around they were coming. So for months the Puritans had nothing to eat but Johnny cakes. Lucky for them, they discovered wild turkey. Now, wild turkeys were stupid birds and easy to catch, even for the Puritans. The Puritans were beside themselves with joy when they discovered wild turkey."

"I'll bet!" It was Chuckles again. "Wild Turkey!" All the bikers started cracking up. I wasn't sure why they were laughing, but I smiled along.

The old man broke in. "This is ridiculous! Turkeys were not stupid birds!"

Everyone stopped and turned. He had turned bright red. Being a person whose skin color made it impossible to blush, I was impressed. Even the Harley bikers stepped back.

"This is the most historically inaccurate, ridiculous tour I have ever seen, even in Salem. Anyone who actually knows American history," he gave me a look, "would know wild turkeys were not stupid birds. They were so intelligent Benjamin Franklin wanted them to be our national bird instead of the eagle."

"What's wrong with eagles?" One of the larger Harley bikers stepped close. I noticed he had an eagle tattooed on his left arm.

"There is nothing wrong with eagles!" This man was on fire. "But I don't enjoy the fact that I paid for a historical tour and have gotten nothing but superficial nonsense!"

I winced. I knew my tour wasn't perfect, but superficial nonsense?

"I teach American History, and almost everything this young lady has said is wrong, wrong, wrong." Each time he said "wrong" his face deepened in color. "It's because of people like her that this country is going to shit."

The hair bristled on the back of my neck. There was an uncomfortable silence for a moment while I took a deep breath. "I'm sorry, sir. I didn't mean to offend you. I'm sure you can get your money back."

"Oh, I'll get more than my money back." He turned and stormed out the door of the Governor's House.

His wife looked embarrassed. "I'm so sorry. He retired early this year, and he just misses teaching history. I enjoyed your tour. Really." Then she ran after him.

Chuckles turned to me. "So where's this frisky old goat you were talking about?"

They all looked at me gently, and suddenly I felt so homesick for Queens, where the men others thought were scary used to be the men who took care of me.

When I got off the tour, one of the other fake Puritans, Walter, was waiting. Walter was tall, thin, and had stringy red hair down to his chin. His face was freckled, and my first thought when I met him was Ichabod Crane, but if Ichabod was a stoner who did gravity bong hits and had a punk band.

We had become friends after I tagged along on one of his tours to see if I could learn any new "facts." His tour was so funny I almost died from not laughing. When we got to the part where there was a fake burial ground, Walter turned to the group and said, "So this is where the Puritans were buried. Of course these wooden posts aren't the original wooden posts. They don't exist anymore. They rotted. Just like the Puritans, and that's why we don't see them much either."

I guess he'd never had that history teacher on his tour.

"Hey Injun." That was Walter's nickname for me. He got a big kick out of the fact that I was Pakistani and working as an English Puritan. "Ron wants to see you."

"Did he tell you about the old guy?"

"Don't worry about it. We get crazies here all the time. Who else would pay for one of our tours?" He had a point.

When I went to the old barn, which doubled as our office, Ron was waiting at his desk. He rubbed his hand over his face. "Razia. I guess you know what this is about."

"The old guy."

"You didn't call him that did you?"

"Of course not." Now it was my turn to be offended. I had more respect for my elders than that.

"Well, that was David Green." I looked blank. "He's one of the board members for the Historical Society in Salem. It's because of him we stay open."

I picked up some trousers which were thrown across the chair, tossed them on the floor, and sat down across the desk from Ron. "I don't think he really enjoyed my tour."

"No, he didn't. He thinks you should be fired."

"Really?"

"He said, well . . ." Ron hesitated. "He didn't think your tour was historically accurate."

"But no one's tour here is historically accurate." I began to feel sick like the time I had eaten one of my own Johnny cakes.

Ron looked embarrassed. Everyone knew he had used the money for our colonial training to have "Ye Olde Keg Party" for the entire staff. He'd insisted Puritans drank a lot of ale. Most of us had gotten so drunk and done such embarrassing things we couldn't even look each other in the eye the next morning.

"Well, he also said your presentation wasn't historically accurate."

"My presentation?"

Ron pulled a soft pack of Camels out of his pocket. He offered me one, but I shook my head and waited.

"The way you look." He lit a cigarette, took a deep drag, then blew it out. "But I talked to him, said you were great, and we agreed you could keep your job. You could be an Indian. I could arrange for a costume, and you wouldn't have to do or say anything. Just stand around. And, you know, act like an Indian."

"But I'm not that kind of Indian."

"I know." He seemed depressed by this fact.

"And it's not like Native Americans were just standing around. They were fighting back. Wait—why are you asking me to do this?"

Ron took a long drag and started having a coughing fit. "Look Razia, we're barely keeping our doors open." He walked to the back door hacking all the way.

"No one cares about Salem pre-witch trials. They come here to hear about the burnings, stonings, hangings, about death. They don't give a shit about what really happened to people when they first got here." Ron spit outside before he continued.

The door looked out onto the ocean, and it occurred to me

that this was the real reason Pioneer Spirit was being taken. Real estate, the oldest colonial reason.

"Why don't you just put me on a stake then? That'll bring people in."

"Razia—"

"Ron. This isn't fair."

He looked at me. I knew he was thinking I didn't look like an English Puritan, but it was one thing to disrespect Puritans and another to disrespect Native Americans.

"Look, think about it." I could see Ron was upset. "Come in the morning and we can talk, okay?"

I didn't say anything. I just walked out the back door and up the dirt road toward the exit, still wearing my costume. It didn't really matter in Salem. You could walk down the street in full seventeenth-century garb, and no one noticed. Half the population did. Everyone was stuck in the past, wearing costumes, pretending they were someone they weren't. I thought of the Harley bikers and my uncles.

And then I thought of my father, the day he told me I had to leave. All too often, his face, ash grey, would rise up in my mind, and each time it would shock me, the way the full moon shocked me when it rose against the buildings in Queens.

I walked faster. Outside the gate, the Harley biker clan was hanging out in the parking lot. They were smoking and passing around a brown bag.

"Hey there, sweetie. Out early?" It was Chuckles and his gang. They looked happy to see me.

"No, I think I just got fired."

There was a general growl. "Fuckers," Chuckles said. And on cue, all of the rest of them spat or mumbled curses. Chuckles passed me the brown paper bag. "Wild Turkey."

I looked inside and laughed, then raised the bag to my mouth and let the whiskey burn through my body. I could taste Chuckles' mouth on the neck.

Crabs
San Francisco, California
February 1995

It started as one of our usual fights. Eric was mad because he'd been standing on the pavement all day, just like any other day, passing out flyers for this psychic who had a shop on O'Farrell off Powell. Eric had to stand on the corner until he had passed out every last one. "So, is she real?" I'd asked Eric when he first got the job.

He was sitting, cutting his toenails on the side of the twin bed we shared in the Barclay Hotel. The bed was pushed up against the wall where the cockroaches liked to crawl at night. The room was so small there was no other place for it, but we weren't complaining. We were living in the Tenderloin in an SRO, but it was still better than living on the street.

I was sitting on the floor, on the dirty carpet. He looked up from his feet and down at me. "Of course she's not real. She's a fucking fake."

I was disappointed. Nothing in San Francisco was turning out to be the promised magic I had dreamed while reading the Beats.

Eric hated the job, but he hated most things. He never finished a full day. Instead, he came home and threw the stack of leftover flyers in our trash. He left early whenever he noticed "the old bag," as he liked to call her, had gone on some errand late in the day "to buy frogs in Chinatown." He always threw the flyers in the small trashcan in our room. I don't know why he didn't just throw them in the garbage can on the street. Maybe he was paranoid the psychic would peer through each can using her powers all up and down Powell and Market to see if he was working, or maybe he just liked it for the dramatic effect.

I knew any day Eric threw the flyers in the trash were bad days for me. The psychic woman did help predict some things. I heard the key turn in the door and then the sound of the flyers being thrown across the room, hitting the side of the garbage, then falling onto the dirty brown carpet. I tensed when I heard his voice.

"Hey, come out here."

I was taking a bath. I'd started to take two or three a day. I'd lost my job at The Garden of Eden, a gourmet shop in the Market Street Mall. It was rough for us now, as I'd stolen almost everything we ate from there. At first I'd felt guilty, but then one evening, the night manager gave me a bag and said, "Fill it up."

The employees of The Garden of Eden treated the store like the Biblical garden where they could eat and drink to their hearts' content. The one time I ever went to the night manager's house, she asked me if I wanted tea, then handed me a menu she'd made listing all the fancy teas she'd stolen. Not surprisingly, The Garden of Eden was going broke. To cut costs, the day manager fired me.

I spent most of the morning looking for work and most of the afternoon and evening in the bathtub. The cold, rainy February of San Francisco had taken over, and it was pouring all the time. I was down to ninety pounds and got dizzy when I walked down the street. We had no money, and I didn't have friends, mostly because Eric got pissed every time I hung out with anyone but him, even if it was other girls. The night manager, who had a crush on me, had invited me over many times, but except for that first night, I'd always been too afraid of Eric to accept. My Muslim father was Gloria Steinem compared to Eric.

I don't know why I had given in to him about the friends thing. It was just easier sometimes not to fight. He always won. He had more stamina, more anger, and maybe he was getting food from somewhere else because he sure as hell always seemed to have more energy. But now it was too late. I felt I had nothing to say to anyone anyway. So I sat all day in the tub letting my skin wrinkle, thinking of my sisters who I wasn't allowed to see.

The bathroom reeked of Pine-Sol, and I wished we had a window that looked out onto the street. When we first got to San Francisco, I walked into the hotel and said to the old man behind the counter, "Is there anything we can rent for eighty dollars?" It was how much we'd come to San Francisco with.

The old man looked at Eric, and then he looked at me. His skin was a faded yellow grey. He came out from behind the counter and led us up the dirty stairs and down a dark hall to a room. When he opened the door, the smell of urine rushed out, and when he turned on the light, cockroaches scattered left and right. The only window in the room looked out onto an airshaft.

"It's yours for eighty dollars a week."

I noticed the bathtub right away. It was one of those old-fashioned ones with feet and a large white porcelain lap. I said, "Yes, we'll take it," before Eric had a chance to say, "No."

But that was a long time ago, when I still felt in control. Now Eric was waiting outside the bathroom door, and I didn't want to come out.

He called from the other room. "Razia! Come out here."

"Wait. Give me a minute."

But a minute was too long for him. The door didn't have a lock. He came and sat on the edge of the bath and put his hand in the water, touching my knee.

I pulled away. The water was getting cold. "Eric stop it."

"You said you were only going to be a minute."

"A minute hasn't passed. I'll be out."

He opened up his fist and I saw a crumpled envelope. "I got a letter. From my mom."

I sighed. He wasn't going to leave. "What's Mom got to say?" His mother lived in Maine with a scary, old hunter in a cabin. Eric and I had lived there too after my parents had kicked me out, and we hadn't yet figured how to get to San Francisco. The hunter had never said a word to me, only grunted for those three terrible months we'd lived in his house.

"Same old shit. How Gus is out with the dogs. How she's sending us some matching sweaters for Christmas."

But I knew there was something else. "What else did she say?"

His face shut down in that peculiar way. "My aunt's telling the whole family how hard it's been for her to help us."

I felt the irritation under my skin. "She hasn't been helping us. We just stayed at her house for two days."

Eric stood up and looked at himself in the dirty mirror, then started patting down his hair. He was vain about his golden curls.

I had liked them, too, once, when we'd first met in a bar back in New York drinking one, two, three beers, two strangers telling each other our dreams of California. Back then, Eric had wooed me with stories of hitchhiking, the beauty of San

Francisco. I'd lapped it all up. I was a year away from finishing college. Then my parents were going to try to marry me to their chosen Pakistani. I needed an escape. I'd only known Eric for two weeks before my parents found out and gave me a choice: come home and get married or never come home again. I'd called their bluff and left.

Eric turned around and looked down at me. "She's complaining about the money."

"The money?" Confusion, then anger flashed through me, turned the bathwater warm for a minute. "What money? How come I've never seen it?"

He ignored my question. "I thought I'd start working and pay her back. But how the hell can I do it with that old psychic bitch keeping me on the street all day? What the hell do you know? All you fucking do is take baths." He was getting more and more worked up. "Why the hell do people in my family talk behind my back? That's what I hate—my mom, my aunt, my grandmother—all they do is sit around all day and fucking gossip." His face was turning red, and he was beginning to clench and unclench his fists.

I suddenly wished I wasn't in the bath, that I had my clothes on. But if I got up, there was no way out of the door except past him. The bathroom was so small the door didn't even close all the way. He reached for me quickly, and I flinched, afraid he was going to hit me. He'd never done it before, but lately I'd started fearing him, edging around.

He laughed when he saw me flinch, then stepped out, still smiling. I sat still, running things through my head. My father had made me choose: the family or Eric. I had thought I was choosing freedom. I pulled the plug in the bath and grabbed my towel.

He was sitting on the bed, packing a bong, the one he'd brought from Maine.

"Where did you get the pot?" We'd been tapped for weeks.

"I told Mary at the pizza shop about the letter, and she gave me a bit of her stash." He looked at me waiting to see if I would get jealous, but I didn't have any energy for his games. I never did get jealous whenever he said things like that. Somewhere in the back of my head, I wished for him to cheat so I could quickly end the relationship.

"Is there enough to share?" I sat down next to him. Maybe there would be peace after all, despite the psychic flyers in the trash. He passed me the bong, and the neon green and pink of the flyers flashed at the sides of my eyes. I leaned. I bent my head forward and sucked. The bong water bubbled. I pulled back and closed my eyes, holding the pot in for a deep breath. I knew there wasn't much, and there wouldn't be any for some time, so I had to hold it, hold onto it. At that moment, it seemed like it was all that mattered. I leaned back.

When I opened my eyes, my brain was already getting a bit fuzzy. Eric was taking another hit and was beginning to get smiley and playful. I was sitting cross-legged. He reached over and started playing with my feet. I smiled. One thing I could say for Eric was that he definitely had a foot fetish, and it was good for someone like me who hated my feet. But then he started touching my legs.

"Eric, stop." I pushed his hand away.

He started kneading my leg. "Oh, come on."

"Really, Eric. I'm not into it." My skin puckered up, and I thought, "Now I'll have to take another bath."

"What's the matter, don't you like me anymore?" He tried to say it like he was being sweet, but below it, I could hear his voice starting to get tense. Before, I would have only heard the sweetness, and I would have fallen under with the guilt, but now I knew better.

For a while, I used to do it just to make him shut up or put him to sleep, but I had reached a point where I just couldn't anymore. The gates of my body were closed. I had to hang out in our tiny room while he masturbated in front of me. I don't know why I didn't leave. Everything just felt frozen inside.

"Come on." He started massaging my leg.

"No, Eric."

But he didn't remove his hand. He kept looking at me, and I could feel his arm tense. Suddenly, he reached over and pushed me down. The bong tipped over, and the bong water spilled and started seeping into the mattress.

"Eric! What? Stop playing! What the hell?" He pulled the towel off me and started trying to get his finger inside. I tried to pull away, but he held me down. "You're wet enough. What? Are you thinking of someone else?"

"I just took a bath, you idiot. Now get the hell off of me." I pushed him away. He didn't resist this time. I got up so fast I almost fell. I was shaking, but I grabbed my pants and shirt off the floor and started putting them on. I had the shirt on backwards, but I didn't care. I snatched my coat and hat. The good thing about that small room was the door was never more than a few feet away.

He had been staring at me almost in shock, but then he started to get up. Maybe he was surprised at himself, at what he'd just done.

"Leave me alone!" My voice cracked it was so hard.

He stood in front of the door. "Look Razia, please stop overreacting."

"Move out of the way." I reached past him for the knob.

He tried to grab my arm, but I pulled away. I was still struggling into my coat as I pushed into the hall.

"Razia, come back!"

But I ran down the hallway. When I turned the corner, I could hear him screaming, "You're such a fucking whore!"

People in the hotel started opening their doors. They stuck their heads out, even though the hotel was full of pimps and prostitutes, and this was nothing new.

"Shut the fuck up!" someone shouted.

I ran down the steps to the lobby and then out the door. I heard Eric behind me. "Razia!" I was afraid he was going to catch me and drag me back, so I slammed out the front and ran as fast as I could. Maybe I was small, but I could run fast.

There was a group of tourists right outside of the hotel, but I just acted like I was running for a trolley. Eric could have run just as fast as me if he had tried. He'd spent four years in the Army and was six foot four. But something must have made him stop. Maybe it was some kind of twinge of integrity or pride. Something that let him know he'd gone too far. He'd gone too far this time.

I ran toward the Embarcadero, past the head shops and coffee shops of Market, until I thought my chest would burst. I ran until the people changed from ragged men lined up outside 25-cent booths to commuters waiting for the trolley to the young rich pretending to be poor hippies and then finally to the older rich in the Financial District who didn't pretend to be poor.

Only then did I slow down.

I was so angry I could boil. If someone held a thermometer against me it would have popped. As I walked through the cold air, toward the getting-colder air of the docks, I could hear the sea lions' voices echoing in the distance.

When I got to the Embarcadero, there was an old man and baby boy. The boy was at the age when he was just beginning to walk. The old man was showing him a crab he'd just caught. The boy's smile nearly pulled off his hat. The old man put the crab into the bucket, but it got out and started splashing around on the wet, getting-wetter dock. The wood was dark with a hollow sound, and the child was laughing, jumping up and down, pointing as the crab scrambled around. The old man laughed, too and bent down next to the child.

I turned around. My heart hurt like a million leagues of ocean pressing up. I thought of my little sisters and how I had left them behind. How I had left everything behind for this world.

Skin
Corona, Queens
August 1983

It had poured rain and thundered all day just like a hot August storm should, and when I opened the door to my friends Lucy's and Saima's house, its glass metal sides tugged on the grapevines. Cooled-down rain, which had pooled on the leaves, showered down on me and wet my salwar kameez.

Lucy lived below Saima, and Saima lived above Lucy, and they both lived next to Shahnaaz, the neighborhood bully. I lived down the street, but in the summers, I spent all my time at Saima's and Lucy's.

The grapevines lived everywhere, acting like they were trees. They grew when our mothers called us in to eat. They grew when we played in the back lot acting like junglees. They grew at night when we were asleep, and in the mornings, we'd push against the door jambs, pull and twist the doorknobs to get out to go to our school, P.S. 19.

The biggest argument Saima and Shahnaaz always had was whose grapevines they really were. They were rooted in Shahnaaz's yard, but most of the vines, with their baby hair twists, hung, swung over the fence and knelt down and touched the ground in Saima's yard.

I always sat on Saima's side of the grapevines, on the red vinyl cushion benches under the trees. Saima I had known since she and I were born, and even before because our fathers had been best friends in Peshawar. They had come to America together with their tight-fitting British suits, curly dark hair, and sunglasses. In Pakistan, they had worn white lab coats. They had been scientists, but in Corona, they worked in stores. Now Saima's father wore tight pants and shiny shirts while he sold radios, VCRs, and illegal copies of Bollywood movies. My father wore his lab coat as a butcher at his Gosht Dukan, Corona Halal Meats. Whenever I visited him, it was covered with blood.

Lucy's father was from the Dominican Republic. He used to work all the time, too, but he had lost his job, Lucy said, because the boss hated Dominicans. Now her father was always outside under the grapevines. He had a fat belly that hung out his wife beater. His hair was white and curly all over his chest. He knew how to make wine, and he'd be drinking wine made from the grapes from last year. Lucy's father yelled at us in his broken English when he saw us popping the sour green grapes into our mouths.

"Hey! You! Get away from my grapes!"

After it rained was the best because Lucy's father would be inside watching TV. Then we'd pull on the vines like hair and feel the rain down our cheeks, soak our clothes, our salwar kameez. It would feel cold, sweet, and green while all the air around us was thick liquid, about to burst like a sneeze.

On one of these summer days, Shahnaaz was poking around in the old abandoned garage that had come with her house. Her family didn't have a car so the garage was left to pile up with junk. It was the kind of place stray cats had babies. The kind of place rats lived. The kind of place you wouldn't go into by yourself, unless you thought you were a bully and a badass like Shahnaaz did.

Our main way of getting money for candy was to look under the cushions of sofas. There the loose change that leaked out of our fathers' and uncles' pockets would slip down and collect into underground pools of pennies, nickels, and dimes. Shahnaaz's brother had just moved an old sofa into the garage, and she thought she had found an undiscovered treasure, but when she lifted the cushion, it wasn't George Washington's head or even Abraham Lincoln's she saw. She saw a woman in a glossy magazine, her nipples pink and round as quarters, her mouth wide open, her head thrown back and nothing on her body but a thin sheet draped over her legs.

Shahnaaz didn't say this, but I'm sure her eyes popped. None of us had breasts, but Shahnaaz always acted like she did, pushing her chest out whenever we walked around the block. She thought she was the prettiest, and the only reason we agreed was because her brother Amir was two years older and would beat us up if we said she wasn't.

When Shahnaaz came up to the fence, Saima and I were sitting under the grapevines pooling our cushion change to see if we could buy candy. Every so often, Saima and I would reach up and pull down a handful of sour green grapes. When we saw her, we weren't happy.

"Whatcha doing?"

"None of your business." Saima had to deal with Shahnaaz more, so she had less patience.

"Oh yeah? Well maybe it is my business because you're eating my grapes."

We rolled our eyes and ignored her, but she continued, "What I found in the garage is none of your business either."

I tried to be tough. "So what then? It's none of our business."

But it was useless. Ten minutes later Shahnaaz was chewing gum and reading the Bazooka Joe comics. I was sneezing from the dust in the garage, and Saima was trying to find a place to sit that wasn't covered with rat pee. Shahnaaz pulled out the magazines, and our mouths dropped open. There was a whole pile of them full of naked men and women in all sorts of positions. Some of them were doing everyday things like eating breakfast, just naked. One woman was spread out on a car.

"Ewww. This is gross," Saima said, but she kept looking. I did, too. I couldn't stop myself from flipping through the pages. I kept the tips of my fingers on the edges, though, so I didn't have to touch the skin. Whenever they accidentally did, I could feel my fingers burning.

There was one lady I couldn't stop looking at. She was the only one who wasn't blonde. She was tall and had dark brown hair and brownish skin. Her body was thin, and she was sprawled out asleep on a bed, completely naked. Her eyebrows were wrinkled, and her hair was messy. There was brown hair, curly and thick, between her legs, brown hair, curly and thick, underneath her arms, in places where my skin was still as smooth as a baby's. The picture must have been taken by someone on top of her. She looked like she was sleeping and having a very bad dream.

"Are they your brother's?" Saima was the first to ask.

"No! My brother would never look at something like this. It's—"

"Guna," I said. A sin. It was what we learned in masjid where our religious teacher, Hafiz Saab, taught us the long lists of what was guna and what wasn't.

It was what we learned at home. "Guna!" my mother always said, especially in the summer when people in our neighborhood walked around wearing almost nothing. "They don't know any better. But you do. You think it's hot now? When you go to Hell, demons will take torches and set fire to all the places you left your skin naked. And as much as you scream and cry, or say please, please, Allah forgive me, Allah will say, 'You didn't listen to me when you were alive, why should I listen to you when you're dead?'" She wiped the counter. "But Allah is merciful, and when the demons have burned you enough, He'll forgive you, give you new skin and bring you up to heaven."

"But how long until I could go to heaven?" I'd say, trying to push the images of demons out of my mind.

"In Hell, every day is an eternity," my mother would say, then leave me to go clean.

"We have to burn them." Shahnaaz's voice was like the voice in my head.

"Saima, does your mother have matches?"

"I don't want to go home. My mother won't let me come back out."

Shahnaaz looked at me. "Razia, go ask the man at the store."

"Why me?"

"Because you're the favorite."

It was true. The bodega owner always gave me free candy whenever I went to buy milk for my mother. She didn't know the bodega was just a front for selling drugs. I didn't either. I just thought it strange that the front windows were full of dish detergent, Ajax, Raid, and Mr. Clean, but the back shelves were barely stocked with anything. The only other thing they sold was milk. At some point, the owner, the man with the gold tooth, must have realized the store could look more legit if they carried dairy. Plus, he could get it cheap for his family. He always said I was his best milk customer, even though I never saw anyone else buying milk there.

When I walked in, the bell rang, and the smell of wet cardboard hit me in the face. Inside, it was ten different shades of dark. A grey cat sat in the corner licking herself. The owner was at the front counter, cleaning his fingernails with a match. His friend, the man with the black moustache, was next to him. They were speaking in low, angry whispers.

The door slammed behind me, and the bell rang loud and frantic. A gold tooth flashed in the dark. "Ah, look who it is. My girlfriend!"

I giggled. The owner's friend grinned, and I could see he was missing his front teeth. He must not have had enough money to replace them with gold.

I quickly asked, "Could I please have a pack of matches?"

The man with the gold tooth passed the matches over the counter. "Baby, what you want matches for?"

I stood on my tiptoes, bit my tongue, and lied, "They're for my father," then mumbled, "Thank you," grabbed the pack, and ran out the door.

When I got back, Saima and Shahnaaz were pulling a metal garbage can into the back alley next to the railroad tracks so the grown-ups couldn't see what we were doing. We had had fire safety training in school and knew we had to be careful. We threw all the magazines in. Shahnaaz insisted she had to light the first match since she had found the magazines.

"But I'm the one who went to get the matches!"

"Yeah, but you'd have nothing to burn if I hadn't found them." Shahnaaz pointed inside the garbage can.

I looked and saw my woman with brown hair still laid out on the bed. I wondered how she had ended up that way. Her mouth looked soft and sad. My mother always told me that it only took one step off the right path to start your downfall. Maybe one step like lying about matches.

"There's only one straight path," my mother always said, "and you need to pray to Allah you stay on it. It's the right path that looks difficult. All the others tempt you, but at the end of each one, there is a trap that drops you into a burning red hot pit of fire with demons."

"But how do you know if you're walking the right path or the wrong path?" I'd ask, trying to push the image of demons out of my mind.

"Listen to what I tell you," my mother would say, and then she'd leave me to go clean.

"Fine. You can light the first match," I said. "Stupidhead," I mumbled under my breath.

Shahnaaz struck the match against the flint and dropped it quickly into the garbage can. We all stepped back, thinking it was going to explode. But it didn't. The magazines were thick and glossy, and the garbage can was damp. We watched as the flame burned, lowered, and then flickered away. Shahnaaz lit match after match, but each one flickered and went out.

"You have to get more matches." She acted all annoyed, as if it was my fault she didn't know how to start a fire.

I didn't argue this time. I wanted the magazines to burn. I ran all the way to the bodega thinking of the woman in the garbage can. Where had she gone wrong? I thought of how easy it was to want to sleep instead of get up to read Fajr namaaz, to want to eat during Ramzaan. I thought of the boys I wanted to kiss: Julio, Phillip, Osman. Is that how it had started for her?

When I got back to the bodega, the man with the gold tooth

was alone, and this time he looked angry. I went to the back first, to the milk fridge, to figure out how to ask him again. If only I had enough money to pretend I was buying milk. The cat was still licking herself.

Finally, I came back to the front and asked, "Could I please have another pack of matches?" The owner looked at me hard. Something crossed his face. "Hey, what are you doing with these matches anyway?"

"They're for my father," I lied again.

"Tell your father he's got to come here himself if he wants matches." Then he looked guilty. He had never said no to anything I asked for before.

"Here." He passed the matches and a square caramel over the counter. "Your favorite."

I thanked him quickly and ran back to the alley behind Saima's house.

"This time I want to light it," I said. When Shahnaaz opened her mouth to argue, I cut her off. "We can't get anymore matches, and you don't know how to light them."

Saima laughed and Shahnaaz gave her a look, but then she stepped back. I stepped up to the garbage can and looked down at my woman. I struck the match and held it to the whole pack, until it became one big flame, a fireball in my hands.

I dropped it right on her. The flame kept and started burning a hole through the center. It turned into a hundred flames shooting up from the silver metal. We could barely see the orange, yellow, and blue of them in the light.

The smoke rose, and the fire reached higher and higher. My woman's skin was beginning to submit, relent. The bed she was on, her sad eyebrows drawn together, her mouth was melting away. Her body was covered with smoke, and I knew her spirit was being lifted so she could fly clothed in fire all the way to heaven.

The Grass Pulled Up
Roadside, Florida
August 1997

The grass pulled up like snakes climbing their way to heaven. My boots were shot. They used to be baby blue, but now they were dirty grey, like a mouse. Natalia was standing in the road hitching, her thumb stuck out, her shoulder turning brown in the sun. Cars kept passing us, and I couldn't believe it. How come no one was picking us up? We were two cute girls, at least I thought, but then I looked at us again and saw two light brown girls made darker from the sun and dust we kept kicking up. We were flying and in love, while an army of mosquitoes happily created trails of blood on our arms.

"Maybe if we don't stand under these trees the mosquitoes will stop bothering us." I looked at Natalia hoping she'd agree.

She lowered her arm and started massaging her shoulder. "We're not having any luck in this place anyway."

We walked down the road a bit, but the mosquitoes had wings and had no problem following.

"If I had one wish," Natalia said, "I'd wish for a bottle of Bug Off."

"Why wouldn't you just wish for all the mosquitoes to die?"

"That's mean!"

"Oh God. I forgot you were a hippie. Well, why not ask for a ride to get us out of here? Or even better, our own car?" I imagined us in a hot, red, topless Bug with the windows rolled down, blasting The Velvet Underground into the lush green of Florida.

"I've got simple needs, Razia, simple needs."

Another car whizzed by. "At least the mosquitoes like us." I tried to slap one off but missed. I looked at Natalia and threw my mosquito-bitten arms around her. It didn't matter about the heat.

Natalia laughed and squirmed but then bit my ear. "More bites!" She pulled me back into the shade of the trees. "Forget these stupid drivers."

She threw herself down on the ground and tried to pull me down with her, but I pulled back. "We can't get dirtier! People with cars probably already think we're going to mess up their seats. Maybe we should stand here with mops so we're more easily recognizable. Third World cleaning ladies."

It was so bad that we both started giggling. So much, we were lucky we heard the car. I heard the sound of wheels from far off first. My head snapped up, and I quickly jumped out into the road and flashed my thumb. By some miracle, the car stopped. It was a Chevrolet and green, like Army but without the camouflage.

I looked back at her. "What do you think?"

"I don't think can walk all the way to Key West."

When we got up to the car, we saw an old man and woman up front. I hesitated. There was a large crucifix with a bleeding Jesus dangling from the rearview mirror. I wasn't used to seeing Jesus a lot, and the sight of him bleeding away was always a bit of a shock.

"Hi!" I said in my perkiest voice, trying not to look at Jesus's scarred body.

"Where you girls heading?" the old man asked. His teeth were denture perfect.

Instinctively, my finger shot up to my one crooked tooth that was always trying to climb over the others and jump out of my mouth. Probably the only chance I would ever have for perfect teeth was going to be when they all fell out and I got dentures. Of course, the way I was living, who knew if I would ever be able to afford dentures, or if I would live that long.

"We're heading to Key West," Natalia said, seeing I was going off into one of my reveries.

"We're heading to Miami, girls. You're welcome to come along." He turned to his wife and said, "Honey, put in those Irish tapes." And she did. We entered the car to the strains of what sounded like pagan Gaelic music.

Natalia and I scooted in like two little children. The seats were clean, a dark olive shiny leather. My sweaty legs immediately stuck to them. I saw the old man looking at us in the rearview mirror. It always happens so fast. One minute you're on the road, and the next minute, you're in a Chevrolet listening to Irish music with an old man and woman who love Jesus. I sat back and started checking them out.

The power dynamics of hitchhiking are weird. In exchange for a ride, you're expected to be entertaining or an open, throbbing, non-judgmental ear. Natalia and I had sat through long tirades about broken marriages and selfish children. We'd listened with mock empathy to one yuppie man's existential despair. We'd heard at least seven stories about how much more fun it had been to hitchhike in the Sixties and how two attractive young girls like us shouldn't be hitchhiking at all.

The old man was wearing a black suit and had heavily-dyed black hair. The woman was wearing a navy blue dress and you could tell she had never, nor would she ever, unless she was hit by lightning or otherwise enlightened, wear pants. I became very aware that Natalia and I were both wearing pretty tight ripped-up jean shorts. Plus, Natalia was wearing a T-shirt that said "Blam!" in large red letters across her chest.

The man's eyes in the rearview mirror were now twice the size they were when we first got into the car. I suddenly knew we had made a mistake. It always amazed me the way some religious people, it doesn't matter what religion they are, go ga-ga over a little bit of skin. It burned me up. The old man's eyes shifted from my face to my breasts then to Natalia's and back. Somehow he still managed to drive straight. I had to give him credit for that.

When I looked over at Natalia, I could tell she was starting to get really upset. She was no naïve cat who had just hit the street. She looked directly into the rearview mirror, and he looked away quickly. His wife didn't seem to notice anything. She just kept changing tapes, listening for half a minute, then popping the cassette out again and replacing it with another tape of unrecognizable music. I guess she didn't like Irish music.

I decided right then and there that I didn't feel like being in a peep show, not to mention one with an indecisive DJ, so I did what I did best. I started talking. "That's quite a crucifix you have," I said. I thought if I brought up the topic of religion the old man might remember some of the commandments. Maybe there was one in there that told you not to ogle young girls.

My plan worked for a second. He started looking at Jesus's naked flesh instead of ours, but then he turned back and looked us up and down as much as that was possible through the rearview mirror.

"Why are you girls heading to Key West?"

"I have a friend there," I said. "She's getting married." It was a lie, but it was better than sharing the truth, that we were on our way to spend time with Natalia's hippie friends who lived in a trailer on the beach.

Plus it was one of our games. Natalia and I would tell fake life stories to the drivers until we started to feel our lies might be real. Maybe we did have parallel lives, ones we'd be able to access as soon as physicists figured out how to move between wormholes.

"Marriage! Is that right? Marriage is one of God's greatest gifts." The old man looked at our thighs as if we were chicken being picked out at a church BBQ. "But where are my manners? My name is John, and this here is my wife, Joy."

I steeled myself before saying our names, but Natalia spoke first.

"I'm Natalia, and this is Razia."

I was grateful to her for absolving me of the first step. You would think it would be a simple exchange, but I'd learned once leaving Queens that saying my name wasn't simple at all.

He looked at us, and I could tell he was weighing our features, deciding which foreign countries we could possibly be from. We could pass for so many. At least he was looking at our faces and not our chests.

Natalia was a mix of many things: Egyptian, Italian, and New England White. In short, she looked more desi than me. Dark and pretty, she got harassed in every gas station and deli. "You Indian? You Pakistani? You Bangladeshi? Will you marry me?" She would roll her eyes and sometimes leave without paying. The men would scream from behind, and she would turn back and say, "Are you that cheap? Well, no then, I won't marry you."

"I'm Pakistani," I said in a clipped tone, hoping he would get the hint but knowing he wouldn't.

"Pakeeestan!" he mispronounced in American. "I was in Karachi in the Seventies." He looked at Joy. "That was before I found the Lord and before I met my better half." Joy paused in her tape pushing and smiled. I could see the precision of her white buck-teeth from the side.

"Partition. Terrible thing the way the natives turned on each other right when the British left!"

Natalia quickly put her hand on my thigh and squeezed my knee to calm me down so I didn't get one of my "Racial Rage Fits," as we jokingly called them.

He noticed our touch, and his face stiffened. Damn, these religious people with their eyes like hawks. You have to be constantly vigilant when you're sitting in the seat of judgment. I caught myself judging. I guess I hadn't shaken off my own religious training.

"Sooooo . . ." he stretched it out like a long, low tire letting out air. "When are your weddings?" He made sure it was plural to avoid any confusion.

Outside of the car, I thought I saw two ostriches running for their lives in the Florida bush. I answered honestly before I could stop myself. "I don't want to get married." It was just a knee-jerk reaction from all the years of answering back to meddling Pakistani aunties who seemed as if they had only one pastime: trying to get the girls in the community married. As soon as they finished with one, they pounced on another. Before the blood was even dry.

"Oh come now." From his voice, I could tell he was going to start preaching, "Marriage is a blessing given to us by our Lord. Haven't you read the Bible?" He didn't wait for a response. "'And the Lord God said, 'It is not good that the man should be alone. I will make a helpmate for him.' That's Genesis."

"Amen," Joy said. I jumped. I had almost forgotten she could speak. I suddenly had a fantasy she was like a blow-up doll who said "Amen" on cue. My skin prickled from the bottom of my neck and into my hair. Was she a doll? She seemed so stiff. I started to worry. Had her "Amen" sounded real or like some kind of cheap playback machine? But then I remembered her changing the tapes.

John winked at us through the rearview mirror. Joy noticed the wink and was roused from her road coma. No, she wasn't a doll.

"It's all in the Bible," she said. "Every direction we need to know for life." She looked over at him with a simpering look, and he glowed down on her with a spark of lust. Oh goodness, they were turning each other on.

"Yes." He reached out a wrinkly hand, one that seemed it had been in a sitz bath for a week, and grabbed her thigh. "The Lord says, 'Therefore shall a man leave his father and his mother, and shall cleave unto his wife. And they shall be one flesh.'"

Natalia looked over at me alarmed. I wasn't feeling too well myself.

Joy turned around, and I nearly jumped. Her face close up was caked with make-up, thick foundation, fuchsia lipstick, and green eye shadow up to her eyebrows. It was scary. I had been so distracted by Jesus and the old man that I hadn't looked at her too closely. She looked from me to Natalia. Her words were covered with spit. "'Marriage is honorable in all, and the bed undefiled, but whoremongers and adulterers God will judge!'"

My stomach felt tight. The air in the car felt impossible to breathe. I wanted to get out, but I didn't know how. This was why I had left my family in the first place, so I would never have to feel this way, trapped and preached to. I pinched Natalia's leg.

"Ow! What are you doing?" she whispered.

"Psychos," I mouthed silently. She nodded, but John thought she was agreeing with him.

"Isn't that right?" He reached over and pinched Joy's thigh hard. She winced and then turned and smiled. I could see her front teeth were coated with lipstick.

"But where are our manners, Joy? Moslems don't believe in our tenets." He shrugged. His whole body loosened, and for a second, in the rearview mirror, he looked like a normal person. "I guess we'll all know what's what on Judgment Day!" He started singing:

The other night as I left the meeting
God's spirit bade me stay
But I said not tonight, for next week only
I must go and dance with the gay.
After that I'll go and get converted
And be a Christian bright
But alas, too late, I see the folly
By saying not tonight.

Natalia and I stared at him. He had no idea how appropriate his song was, but more than that, John's voice was shockingly beautiful. Suddenly, I felt jealous. I'd never been allowed to sing myself. It was forbidden in my Orthodox family. Not knowing what to do with the heat of my feelings, I rolled down the window. The air felt cool and fresh, wet, full of sweet smells I didn't recognize, ones I wanted to breathe in.

John abruptly ended the hymn and began to scream. "What are you doing?! Can't you see the AC is on?"

I heard the sound of Irish flutes being dragged through mountain passes and Joy mutter something under her breath. I thought I heard "Heathens" and suddenly missed the mosquitoes like they were long lost friends.

"Careful." Natalia put her hand near my thigh. I bit down on my lip.

But that was it. I started looking along the side of the road for a sign. Then I saw one. "Food Gas Lodging," a blue square against the wet Florida green.

"I'm not feeling well. Maybe we should pull over. You can drop us off at the next rest stop."

"Oh no-no-no-no-no-no." He shook his head vigorously. "I said I was going to take you to Miami, and I'm going to take you to Miami. Besides, two young girls like you shouldn't be hitchhiking. I wouldn't be able to forgive myself if I left you back on the road for any sick person to pick up." He nodded gravely.

Joy backed him up with an "Amen." Was that the kind of thing someone said "Amen" to? I didn't think so. John looked at her sharply. I guess it wasn't. Joy fidgeted in her seat, and I felt her shrink into herself. She started changing tapes again, putting one in, listening for a minute, and then switching it out.

Outside, Florida was waving by us. Lizards stuck out their tongues, and millions of insects buzzed.

"Does your family know you're hitchhiking? That you're out here?" He looked at me through slit eyes. I got a chill down my spine and not one from the AC either.

Of course no one really knew where we were. We hadn't told anyone we were hitchhiking. For the first time, real panic, not just the slight intimation of it, hit me.

He gave me a sick smile. "I wouldn't think people from your country would allow their daughters to go hitchhiking."

My heart contracted. I looked over at Natalia and felt an overwhelming desire to protect her from the world. Even though it would probably be the other way around. I started formulating a plan. It was something my health teacher had told me to do if I was ever in danger.

Natalia looked straight into his eyes through the rearview mirror. "The first hitchhikers were just travelers who hopped onto caravans on the Silk Road. Didn't you know?"

John laughed. "Is that so?" His eyes shifted to Natalia to get another look at her breasts.

I took the opportunity, leaned forward, stuck my finger down my throat. The bagels and butter Natalia and I had eaten in the morning came up fast.

The man and his dentures started rattling. Vomit had gotten on his black suit. "Jesus Christ!" Joy gave him a swift look, but it didn't stop him. "Why didn't you tell us you were feeling sick?"

"She did," Natalia said. She looked worried until I winked. She shook her head, then looked at him. "We're sorry, really sorry. Could we just pull over at this rest stop?" The exit was right there. "We'll help you clean up."

Yeah right, we were going to help them clean up. Natalia and I were going to scram as soon as we could, leaving John and his wife in the parking lot wondering why it was taking us so long to get paper towels from the bathroom. That car was going to stink all the way to Miami, and we were going to hop into the back of a Pepsi truck where the driver would let us sleep in peace for hours.

As we took the exit, he was fuming. The backs of his ears were red. He wasn't looking at us anymore as he drove his olive green Chevrolet down the ramp. Natalia looked at me and smiled. I looked at her, wiped my mouth, and smiled back.

The Summer of Young Uncles
Corona, Queens
August 1982

It was the summer of young uncles. Somewhere in some office in Pakistan, the go ahead was given. Or maybe somewhere in some office, someone who didn't follow the rules, or only followed the rules of his wallet, was given a promotion so in villages all over Pakistan, young boys who had been surly teenagers kicking crows on dirt roads had turned into men. Moustaches burst onto their faces. Heads burst out of the ceilings of their houses. Enough airmail letters crisscrossed the Atlantic. Enough mothers and wives were consulted or told. Feelings of happiness and concern passed through their faces. Permission was given or not given and young Pakistani men flooded the streets of Corona.

That summer, all of Saima's uncles began appearing. They were like those Russian nesting dolls made out of the same mold: some with red moustaches, some with brown, some short, some skinny, some fat, but they all had the same look. They were Pathans: white skin, handlebar moustaches, and like all Pathans, they carried their sex around with them like wild cats. A few paired up with overweight Dominican and Italian women who had been in the country longer. The uncles needed green cards, and they needed them fast.

I would see a handsome uncle, a man who looked like he could live in the pages of a magazine, and he would be with a woman as large and beautiful as an air balloon. She'd bend down and say, "Oh she's so cute." I'd pull away. I wasn't used to that kind of adult attention. When I'd see the uncles with their ladies coming, I'd run and hide.

I felt guilty, even back then. I knew something wrong was going on. These women loved the Pakistani uncles. They bought them new clothes, sunglasses, and shoes. In exchange, the uncles walked with them down the street, their eyes wandering to all the younger girls who were off limits. Next to their beds were picture frames of the women they had married or were supposed to be marrying back in Pakistan.

Saima's most handsome uncle, Azim, got a job at my father's Gosht Dukan. My father owned a butcher shop called Corona Halal Meats. It was on the corner of 99th and National Street. Before it was a Halal meat store, it had been an Italian butcher shop, and even though my father didn't hang sausages and pigs' heads out front, the meaning was the same. Dead animals arrived there to be cut, sold, and eaten.

It was fine real estate for religion on National Street. The Jehovah's Witness, an Episcopalian church, and our masjid were crammed next to each other, wall to wall, skin to skin. And, if you crossed the street, there was a Catholic store selling crucifixes and paintings of women and men in hell burning. The sinners looked like all of us, but I always thought all of us in our agony looked like Jesus.

It was only right then that there should a place for animal sacrifice as well. There could have been people slaughtering goats on that very spot for centuries. Men might have gathered, talked, and joked, the smell of blood and flesh making their jokes funnier, just like it did in the Gosht Dukan.

My mother always gave me tea to take to the store around four o'clock. It was one of my favorite things to do because I loved visiting my father. In this country, with so few people to love, he'd showered me with affection until even my mother and neighbors said I would get spoiled.

On the front door of the Gosht Dukan there was a dirty sign that said OPEN and another that said OUT FOR PRAYER. A bell rang when I entered. My father looked up and smiled a smile as large as an onion rack. He was standing at the back by the register with Yaqeen Uncle and Azim. Yaqeen Uncle worked as a mechanic in the gas station across the street. He always came at this time because he knew he would get free tea. He was sitting in one of the collapsible chairs my father had especially for him.

"Shafiq Saab!" Yaqeen Uncle tossed a bag of pistachios at my father. It landed on the counter. I knew he wasn't going to pay for it. Azim looked to see if it was okay, but my father didn't hesitate. He opened the pistachios and passed the bag to Yaqeen Uncle. Azim brought out a plate. My father took the kettle from me, and Azim pulled a bag of Styrofoam cups from the shelf. My father poured full cups for Yaqeen Uncle and then Azim. There was only half a cup left for my father at the end. Only I noticed this. The uncles didn't.

Yaqeen Uncle started on one of his favorite subjects: Comparative Religion. "The Yuhovah's Witnesses came to the Garage!" Bits of pistachio fell out of his mouth. Some of the shells missed and fell to the floor.

Azim got out the broom to sweep them up. "Why are they called that? Did they witness something?"

My father laughed. He brought out the sugar, a half-pound bag torn open at the top. It had a hot-pink label and a plastic spoon with tea-soaked sugar crusted along the edge. Then he reached under the counter and brought out a pamphlet that said

"Awake!"

"They gave it to me when they came to the Gosht Dukan. I tried to give them my Quran, but they wouldn't take it."

Azim and Yaqeen Uncle started laughing. I giggled, too. I was usually quiet around the uncles, happy just to be near my father, a little planet circling about. But this time I said, "They don't celebrate Christmas." My father looked over at me and smiled.

Yaqeen Uncle grabbed the spoon and loaded his cup full of sugar, then took a loud slurp from his chai. "This Christmas, I finally understand, but Easter—"

"I know Easter," my father said. "Easter is when Jesus goes upstate."

We all looked at him. My father's English was sometimes a little confused.

"Upstate kaisey? Bus pey?" Yaqeen Uncle smiled.

My father pointed his chai cup in the air. "Upstairs, up-stairs."

"Upstairs, acha," and they both started laughing.

Azim, who had only been in the country for a few months, looked at them, then asked in all seriousness, "But what do eggs have to do with it?"

They were all laughing so hard, they didn't hear the door chime and Hafiz Saab walk in. My father looked up, and everyone quieted down and said salaam.

Hafiz Saab was our imam. Before he came, we children would run wild on the streets, but after, we were rounded up and sent to the basement of the masjid to learn Quran. Hafiz Saab had just come from Pakistan, but he might as well have come from a different planet, he was so strange to us. But to our parents, looking at him reminded them of home. The men would slap him on the back and follow him around like lost puppies, and the women would hide behind doors and giggle whenever he passed.

"Here's Hafiz Saab. Ask him." Yaqeen Uncle got up from his chair and offered it.

Azim, who hadn't touched his chai yet, handed his over. "Hafiz Saab, what is it that the Yuhovahs witness?"

Hafiz Saab's lips puckered. He said in Punjabi, "Don't make yourself crazy thinking about these things. Learn a little bit about Islam, why don't you?"

Everyone looked down guilty. "Haan haan, yeh to hai." That is what they paid Hafiz Saab for, to keep them in line.

He sipped on his chai. "Ek chicken kaat key dey do."

My father went into the back and sifted through the parts of chicken to give Hafiz Saab his favorite pieces: four legs, three necks, no breasts. He threw these into a plastic bag where the blood clung to the inside edges. Hafiz Saab took the bag of chicken, wet and floppy.

He made a half-gesture to look in his pants pocket. Hafiz Saab had started a new fashion among the uncles, a salwar on top and pants on the bottom. That way, they could still look Pakistani, but have pockets for all the things necessary to carry in this new country: keys, identification cards, money. All the men had started to dress like Hafiz Saab. All except Saima's uncles. They still wore tight jeans and shiny, polyester shirts.

After coming up empty-handed, Hafiz Saab looked at my father. "Write it in The Book." My father didn't hesitate. He pulled out The Book. For Pakistanis in Corona, there were two books. One was the Quran and the other was where my father fed everyone in the community for free. If my mother ever found out about The Book, she would go crazy. What everyone owed was written down in there.

At first, people only owed small amounts, but when they realized my father was never going to ask them for payment, the sums got larger, and the items went from packs of roti to burlap sacks of flour. From half a chicken to a whole goat. It was all written at first in my father's flowing handwriting, but now it was written in Azim's. It was hard to tell the difference. To me, all men in Pakistan had the same script.

"Chalo, it's time for namaaz." Hafiz Saab took one last long sip and put his cup down on a shelf next to the counter. He didn't bother to throw it in the garbage, even though it was right next to his feet.

I drifted to the back of the store, touching bags of all different kinds of daal by color. My father called me back to the front. "Do you want to come with me?"

I nodded excitedly, and everyone laughed. The masjid had just gotten speakers, and Hafiz Saab was going to give the azan so the whole neighborhood could hear. The masjid wasn't even close to finished, but our fathers had started from the top and were building their way down.

"Azim, go on ahead," my father said.

The uncles and Hafiz Saab left. I waited while my father threw away the cups and put the towel back on the tea kettle, then put it where the mice couldn't reach. He locked the door and turned the sign to OUT TO PRAYER. We walked to the masjid together, quiet, the way we always were when we were alone.

It was Maghrib time and the light was dimming. The sky

was turning from blue to orange to pink. We heard Hafiz Saab even before we got there. I didn't know his voice could sound like that, like a man's voice turning back into a boy's. He recited into the air, "Allah ho Akbar . . . Allah ho Akbar. . . ."

The azan came through over the loudspeakers. Men and women everywhere came out on the street. Everyone in the neighborhood tilted their heads and listened. Out of basement apartments and sixth-floor walkups, Muslim men started walking toward the sound, pulling their topis out of the backseats of their pockets.

The sun went down, and the clouds bent low over the buildings. I stood in front of the masjid and held my father's hand. The light was turning pink and darkening, and I saw my father was weeping as a sleepy, blue light settled on everything.

The Old Italian
Corona, Queens
August 1983

Saima's house was crammed up next to the train tracks, and every time one passed, it would blast through, blowing garbage and letting its long, wild siren blow in the air. The houses were all by the tracks like this:

railroadtracksrailroadtracksrailroadtracks

Saima's house   Shahnaaz's house
Lucy's house   Old Italian's house

When Saima and I ran outside, a train was just passing. The sound of her little brother Ziyad screaming was behind us, and we saw Lucy and Shahnaaz were already hanging out in the front yard under the grapevines. Ziyad was screaming because his mother was forcing tablespoons of hot chili powder into his mouth. Who knows what Ziyad had done or not done this time to make her angry.

It was hot hot hot. Lucy was sitting on a milk crate snapping gum and flipping her long dark hair. She was wearing short shorts. Her belly was chubby as cake and pushed through her T-shirt. Shahnaaz was lying out flat, hogging the entire sofa Lucy's mother had put out under the grapevines.

All over Corona, there were sofas like this, growing like mushrooms in our front yards, yellow, red, orange, brown. Who could get rid of a sofa after paying so much? This one was red vinyl, and I could hear Shahnaaz's skin unstick when she got up.

"I'm bored," Shahnaaz said when she saw us.

"I'm bored too," Lucy said.

"I'm bored three," Saima said. "Move over." She pushed Shahnaaz's skinny legs over to the side.

"Whadda you want to do?" Shahnaaz asked. She must have been too hot to start a fight. No one answered for a few minutes.

"We could go get some ices," I suggested.

"Anyone got money?" Lucy looked around, but we all shook our heads no. We were too young to work and our families too poor to give us allowance. Any money we had was money we found.

We heard the sound of Ziyad crying from one floor up.

"You know when Amir crashed his bike into the fence?" Shahnaaz asked.

"Yeah, so?" we said. None of us liked Shahnaaz's bully brother Amir.

"So, stupid, there's a hole so we can look into the Old Italian's yard."

The Old Italian's yard was a field of sunflowers. He had started planting them years ago, crowding up each seed next to another, and now the sunflowers grew so close, so tall, we could see their heads bend over the fence. On warm days in the summer, the Old Italian wandered through his garden, a floating head among the flowers. But mostly he leaned out from his second-floor window, smoking his pipe and letting his belly hang out, watching whatever was going on in the neighborhood, the new Halal meat stores and Dominican mothers pushing wheelie carts.

Our neighborhood was a hand-me-down from the Italians.

When we moved in, most of them moved out. But some of the old ones hadn't left. They sat on stoops with milky-white skin and let the sun drip over them, or they hid behind doorways with stacks of old newspapers and cold salads. They watched us all the time, frowning. They'd spent a generation planting and creating gardens out of the hard rock soil of Queens. When Italians lived there, gardenias and roses grew. Cherry trees and magnolias burst from the ground. But in our hands, these same gardens filled up with weeds, old sofas, and rusty cars.

Saima reached over her head and snapped some grapes off the vine. There were a few that had turned purple and sweet. Then she jumped up. "Let's go."

We were all experts at climbing fences. In a few minutes we had climbed into Shahnaaz's yard and were pushing against each other to press our eyes against the crack, a broken knot in the Old Italian's fence the size of a fist. The light moved through the flowers like lions set loose in Queens.

Then I saw the Old Italian. Up close, he was a giant. There were puffs of white hair around his smooth, bald head. His face was sun burnt, cracked. He was wearing a white tank top, and it made his skin look older. The knees of his pants were worn from bending down in the dirt. He poured water, and it caught the light. The sunflowers stiffened and straightened.

Lucy was the first to see the small brown shoebox at his feet. "Whaddya think's in that box?" she whispered, then pressed her body closer to the fence.

"Maybe a dead baby," Shahnaaz said.

"Don't be stupid. It's a shoebox. He's probably got shoes in it. And stop hogging already." Saima pulled Lucy and Shahnaaz out of the way.

"It could be a really small baby," Lucy said.

All of a sudden, Saima screamed and pushed back so fast we fell over. The Old Italian's eye was pressed into the crack looking back at us. Just as quick as it had come, his eye disappeared.

"Great idea, Shahnaaz," Lucy said as she dusted off her legs. She was starting to grow hair on her calves. It was still light brown, but I could see it as her skin got dark in the summer.

Shahnaaz straightened her skinny body up. "Whatever. I'm not scared of him. Let him come over here."

"Oh yeah? What would you do?" Saima's salwar had also gotten dirt on it, and she was quickly trying to rub it off. I knew her mother would not be happy about cleaning another dirty salwar.

While we were arguing, the Old Italian had walked around the corner and come in through Shahnaaz's fence. He walked slowly with a limp. His pants were blue, splattered with paint, his belly big as if he was pregnant. The heat was pushing off the cement. I heard cicadas and the sound of the train over them. He held the shoebox out to us and spoke with a thick accent. "Hallo."

"Hello," we mumbled as if we were in school, getting shy all of a sudden.

We gathered around the box, and this time we didn't push. It was lined with newspaper, and in the center, there was a grey kitten. She was so tiny that she could've fit into my palm. Her fur puffed up all around her like a dusty halo.

"She hides in the flowers," he said.

We looked up at him. We had all become mute with the kitten so close. I had never seen a kitten in real life, only on the Scholastic posters my family couldn't afford to buy. I reached out to touch her softness. She was grey as a cloud on a thundery day, as the balls of wool that settled under the furniture of Saima's house. When I touched her, a spark of electricity flew in through my fingers, and the world around me came into focus. I saw the chain links of the fence, the weeds that grew everywhere in Shahnaaz's and Saima's yards. Everything compared to the kitten felt harsh, dirty, brown, covered with bad graffiti.

It was the first time the Old Italian had ever spoken to us. "You wan' her?"

"Oh yes, yes, yes," we said.

He grunted, relieved we had finally spoken. And just like that, he became uncomfortable. He placed the box down under the grapevines and walked out through the fence and back to his garden.

Like a pressure cooker bursting, everyone started talking at once.

"Stop touching her!"

"You stop touching her!"

Soon we all were fighting.

"You're scaring her!" Lucy yelled, and the kitten jumped inside the box. She was shivering.

I turned to Lucy. "Can you bring milk?" Only Lucy could go into her fridge without her mother yelling.

Lucy hesitated, but then she said, "Only if one of you come."

Saima and Shahnaaz both looked at me. Lucy was Dominican, and our mothers wouldn't let us into anyone's house who wasn't Pakistani, but I lived two blocks away, so my mother was the least likely to find out. Besides, Lucy was my friend.

There was a door that had once connected the two yards, but it had rusted shut so we always had to climb the fence when we went between Saima's and Shahnaaz's. My salwar snagged and ripped on a chain link. My mother was not going to be happy.

Inside Lucy's house, everything was different than I imagined. The way Saima's mother described it, I thought there were fountains of beer and drugs everywhere. I didn't know what drugs looked like, though, so while Lucy went into the kitchen, I looked around, searching for something that might be drugs.

There was an old table fan going in the living room blowing hot air around. There were orange sofas with plastic, a TV with aluminum foil on the antenna, books, newspapers, and shoes scattered around the brown carpet. It could have been anyone's house. When I went into the kitchen behind Lucy, I saw they even had the same fridge as Saima. When Lucy opened it up, there was beer inside, and for some reason, I felt better.

"We better hurry. My mother's still in the bedroom putting her face on."

Before I could ask what that meant, I heard her mother call out, "Lucy?"

Lucy didn't answer, but she should've because just then her mother came in. She must have been getting ready to go out. Her hair was all in pink curlers and her make-up was half-on, half-off. Lucy was just about to pour some milk into a cracked cereal bowl. Her mother smiled at me, then looked at Lucy and said something in Spanish. Lucy started talking to her mother.

I looked back and forth between them. From Lucy's hands, the way she moved them around, I could tell she was telling her mother about the kitten. Her mother's smile got tighter and tighter then finally snapped and fell apart. She said something else. Lucy looked at me as if to say: it's time to leave.

When we walked out, Lucy carried the bowl carefully. There was just a little milk in it, but it was enough for now. I climbed over the fence first. Lucy passed the bowl to me and then climbed over.

"How would it feel, do you think," I asked, "if you lost your mother?"

Lucy didn't answer. She concentrated on how to get her bare legs over the fence.

I decided not to ask her what her mother had said. Even with Saima and Ziyad's mother, I never asked. She was always yelling in Pashto, and I knew it wasn't nice.

When we got back to Shahnaaz's yard, Saima and Shahnaaz were still playing with the kitten. Saima was saying "meow" over and over, trying to speak in the kitten's language.

There wasn't enough room in the shoebox for the bowl. Everyone else was too scared to do it, so I lifted her out of the box. I could feel her small bones in my hand. I put her under the grapevines, and we watched as she explored the dirt and sticks scattered there. The kitten was still shivering, but when we put the bowl of milk next to her, her pink tongue came out like a snail.

I don't know how the whole day passed, but we couldn't feel the heat anymore. We spent the entire afternoon with the kitten. Saima, Shahnaaz, and I wanted to give her a Muslim name, but Lucy wanted to give her a Catholic name like Maria.

We finally settled on Maria Perez Parvez Mirza, but since that was too long, we just called her Miss Kitten.

We decided Lucy had to beg her mother to keep it. It had to be Lucy because we were Muslim and everyone knew Muslims didn't have pets. Lucy looked doubtful, but she said she'd try.

The next morning, I was up early, and after eating nashta, my mother gave me permission to go back. When I got to Saima's and Lucy's, Lucy was under the grapevines. The front of her T-shirt was wet with tears. By her feet was Miss Kitten's box, but I didn't hear any kitten sounds. I looked in the box. It was empty.

"What happened to Miss Kitten?"

Lucy didn't answer. She ran inside and slammed her door. I rang Saima's doorbell, but no one answered. Then I heard the sound of the train coming from the back alley next to the railroad tracks. I knew I shouldn't follow it, but I did.

At the end of the alley there was a group of kids. Saima's brother Ziyad and his friend Nelson were in the center. There was a circle of blood at their feet. Ziyad was holding what looked like a rat in his hands.

The children were yelling, "Throw it! Throw it!"

"Ziyad!" I was only a few years older than him, but in our families this still had some power. "Ziyad!"

He turned and looked at me. There was terror in his face. I must have sounded like his mother. But the crowd was pushing now. He turned his back on me and arched his arm. I saw it was our kitten in his hands. Her body sailed through the air and landed on the railroad tracks.

She could have still been living when the train came.

"Ziyad!" I screamed and ran to grab him, but all the boys scattered and ran down the alley laughing. "Ziyad! Ziyad!" My voice sounded like nothing under the tracks of the screaming train.

When I walked back, my throat felt like it had a rope tied around it. The Old Italian had heard the noise and limped out into the back alley. He was looking at the ring of blood on the cement. The horrible feeling in my stomach felt like vomit. The Old Italian looked at me, and the concern left his face. It became filled with the look I saw from all the other Italians. A look of hate.

Then I knew they were right. We were bad. We were as dirty as all the Old Italians said. We didn't know how to take care of life. We didn't know how to grow anything, and when we touched the world, it died.

G-TV
New Rochelle, New York
October 2000–October 2001

i. Three Pine Trees, October 2000

There are three pine trees growing in front of 22 Forest Avenue. Every other house on the block is open. There are front yards more well-kept than baseball fields. There are tulips and rose bushes and Italian men who get up every morning to take care of them. Their yards are like well-kept Caddies and their Caddies are like well-kept yards. It's all the same to them. But at 22 Forest, the pine trees cover the house, and there is a garden made of stone. I live here with the Russo family. They call me Razeeah.

Behind the pine trees, there is a statue of an old dwarf man who stands at the door and a fountain Valerio, the father, likes because the little angel has his hands between his legs. Valerio's the one brother in the Russo clan (there are twelve of them in all) who is a fallen Catholic, but he still loves statues. At least once a week, Leo, Valerio's brother who lives down the street, comes over to argue. They stand on the wrap-around porch covered by the trees, their voices jumping around in the stone and fir. They smoke Winstons and yell at each other about Jesus.

Valerio says, "Fuck Jesus for what he did to Angela." She's his daughter who's been in the hospital for years.

Leo says, "God will strike you down right on this porch if you say that again." But God never does.

And they are there almost every morning. When I walk

outside, they stop arguing for a second, become pleasant, say hello, smile, and ask me how I'm doing. But when I am no more than halfway down the block, I can hear their voices raised high again, cursing.

I am what you would have called in the old days a boarder, a young girl who rents out the attic of a too-large Victorian house. The Russo children used to play here when they were young, but when their mother died years ago, Valerio started renting it out, and the children had to grow up. When I moved in, Tony, the son, was the only one who was still around. I avoided him for the first year because he reminded me of the dangerous Italian boys from my block back in Queens.

Then there was one night when I was walking home from school. The dry autumn leaves crunched gravel under foot. I saw Tony standing under the fir trees smoking with his friends, Victor and Benny. I smelled a certain familiar smell and realized they weren't smoking cigarettes.

"Something smells good," I said to them. They started laughing. After that, I was a regular on the porch.

ii. Breaking Balls, October 2001

"Go ahead Benny. Break my fucking balls."

As usual they were waking up the whole neighborhood. Tony was leaning against the railing, smoking a cigarette, his dark black hair slicked into little points. He was strikingly handsome like one of those tanned, muscular guys on the cover of *Men's Health*. His face lit up when he saw me.

"What are you guys doing out here?" I asked. "I can hear you cackling from my window."

They all raised their beers in greeting. Benny grabbed his fast before Victor picked it up. Victor had a bad habit of taking sips from everyone else's beers.

"Victor, stop being a pussy and drink your own beer."

"Hey!" Victor pointed at Benny, then Tony. "Fuck you and fuck you." He looked at me and opened his arms. "Razeeah, how ya doin?" I was never sure what Victor thought of me, but he was being friendly tonight, so I hugged him. He was solid muscle and smelled of cigarettes and expensive cologne. "Where the hell have you been? We've been out here since ten."

"I was writing." And I had been, but I couldn't concentrate with them laughing outside.

Tony blew a stream of smoke into the air. "Razeeah. Damn you. You're always writing." He took it personally because it meant I wasn't hanging with him.

"I am damned already," I said. I felt it because the writing wasn't working. It seemed pointless with everything going on in the world. I sat down on one of the empty plastic chairs next to Benny. "Hey, I need some advice." I pulled out a cigarette, and Benny paused in his sulking to hand me his lighter. He could be a gentleman when he wanted.

"Razeeah. Is someone giving you trouble? 'Cause you know we'll take care of them."

"Kind of. I want to go to this protest in Washington, for Afghanistan, but I'm scared. I don't know if I should go. I'd be going with a Palestinian contingent."

Victor broke in. "Damn Razeeah. I'd be scared too."

"No! I'm not scared of them. I'm scared we'll all be arrested and deported."

"Razeeah," Tony said, "Why don't you do what my girl Maria does?"

"Your girl Maria?" I thought of her. She was a Queens girl after my own heart. But unlike me, she was one of the sexy ones with straightened, highlighted hair, dark, beautiful eyes, a golden brown tan, nails, three-inch heels, and a voice attached to a megaphone. Whenever she came on the weekends, she taught me how to put on make-up.

"Maria is protesting?" I was confused, imagining her marching in stilettos.

"Yeah. Maria, she doesn't go to Arab stores anymore. She's boycotting them."

I bit my lip. "Ummm . . . that wasn't the kind of protest I was talking about."

Victor laughed. "Tony, you idiot! It's people like you she's going to protest against."

Tony looked at me, and when he did, he was smiling. "Damn you Razeeah! You're going all the way to Washington to protest against me?"

The only thing Tony loved more than Maria was his Caddy. Valerio had found it for him for cheap, but it was wrecked. Tony and Benny spent the whole summer fixing it up. They tinted the windows, redid the interiors, souped up the engine, and put on the shiniest, fanciest rims I'd ever seen, even in Queens.

Tony spent every weekend cleaning and waxing his Caddy while I sat on the porch reading books on feminist politics. Sometimes I looked up the block and saw Italian men of all ages in their driveways, their undershirts glinting in the air, slick green hoses out, cleaning and waxing their cars, the sun shining just right off the hoods.

After Tony finished, we usually went for a ride around town. Once I was telling him about where I grew up in Queens. I took a hit and held it in, then blew it out. "It was fucked up. You never knew when you were going to get jumped by people you thought were your friends or your friendly neighbors. It was like a racist food chain. There were the Italians, the Dominicans, the Puerto Ricans, the Ecuadorians, the Columbians, the Cubans, the Koreans—"

"The Mexicans?" In New Rochelle, the ethnic war was between the Italians and the Mexicans.

"No. There weren't a lot of Mexicans. But Pakistanis were on the bottom of the chain. We were the nerdy wimps. Everyone could beat us up. It's worse now."

"Where were the Italians?"

"Do you have to ask?"

"Hey!" He honked the horn in joy.

"Tony."

"There was a pretty girl."

"But really, are you listening? My friend's little brother would come home and both his eyes would be blacked out."

"Razeeah, that's fucked up. I wouldn't even do that to a Mexican."

I gave him a look. In the beginning, I used to lecture him, and he had at least stopped saying things in front of my Mexican friend Cecilia.

"I'd let them keep one eye for riding their bikes to make deliveries. Hey!" He honked the horn again.

"Tony—" I passed the joint to him. My voice choked up. "You're an idiot. You know, the boys in my neighborhood can't even go to the masjid anymore without being harassed, sometimes jumped. One of my neighbor's brothers was just beaten so bad with a baseball bat he's still not conscious."

Tony took a hit, keeping his eyes on the road. "Shit, Razeeah." I could see he was thinking. "Is that why you're against racism?"

Later that night, Victor brought over his bong and me, Tony and him were taking hits. Benny was over, but he was sulking in the corner. The porch topic for the evening was porn.

"Razeeah," Tony said, "I'm not one of those sick fucks who watches porn all the time. I was just telling my girl Maria, sometimes when I can't see her, I gotta find some way to release the pressure."

"I don't think it's sick. I was in porn once."

"You were?" Suddenly all of them, Tony, Victor, and even Benny sat up.

"It was this film about safe sex for queers."

They looked disappointed.

"Damn Razeeah," Victor said, and then they all started laughing and hollering.

"What?" I knew they were laughing at me.

"Razeeah, even when you do porn, it's gotta be porno for the fucking dolphins."

iii. Bombing, October 2001

The protest happened, but Afghanistan was bombed again and again. Valerio had become a news junkie and would have all three TVs on at once. When he had to leave the house for any reason, he had a news radio he kept plugged in his ear.

I thanked God that out of all the Italian homes I could have lived in, I had found the one house whose patriarch was an anarchist. We were the only ones who didn't have an American flag on the door, even though neighbors regularly came by and left them in our mailbox.

Johnny, the senior, our next-door neighbor, rang the doorbell and even hung around until Valerio put up the flag. But after Johnny left, Valerio ripped it off and threw it behind the bushes.

"Razeeah, those motherfuckers, excuse my language, those cocksuckers tried to draft me when I first got here."

"They tried to draft you?" I looked at Valerio. He was in his sixties, but he looked eighty because he didn't take care of himself. He didn't have any front teeth. His skin was brown from the sun or not bathing, and he was always drunk off Carlo Rossi.

I repeated my question a little louder because he was also slightly deaf. "They tried to draft you?"

"Yeah, when I came from Italy, they tried to draft me for

Corona

Vietnam."

"What did you do?"

"I told those assholes I didn't speak English."

I laughed and thanked God for Valerio who had become the alcoholic father I had never had.

Benny came by later around midnight. Victor had left, but me and Tony were still sitting on the porch, joking and smoking. Benny was a seven-year-old trapped in a man's body. He threw temper tantrums the whole neighborhood could hear. He spent his time playing video games or breaking things for no reason. Stringing together a few sentences was beyond him, but he was a genius when it came to fixing cars and roofs. He was over all the time, but Tony never asked him to leave, partly because he was Tony's best friend Johnny's little brother and partly because there was always a car or roof to be fixed.

When Benny started a story, me and Tony would do whatever we could to change the subject because it would be so painful to listen. But today he actually had something to say. "They're sending Johnny." Johnny had been in the Navy for the last few years.

Tony and I both turned to him. Tony took a drag off his cigarette. "You sure?"

"No, I'm telling a fucking riddle."

"Why the hell didn't he call me?"

Benny shrugged. He started tearing at the branches that hung over the porch. Valerio had planted three evergreens back in the Sixties. Now they loomed over the house and covered our illegal porch activities from the rest of the neighborhood.

Every other house had open, well-mown lawns, tulips, and roses. We had a dark evergreen wall.

"We should just nuke those fucking Arab shits and get it over with," Benny said.

I sucked in my breath. I'd gotten used to the curses and the racist jokes. But Benny wasn't joking this time. And it hit me. I had underestimated him. Benny was an idiot, but it was idiots like him who held our fate in their hands.

Tony was angrier than I'd ever seen him. "Benny, you fuck. That's Razeeah's family you're talking about." It wasn't my family, but it was close enough.

Benny looked at me. Maybe he was seeing me for the first time. He spit off the side of the porch, threw his lit cigarette in the garden, and stormed off, his boots roughing up the steps. He got into his car, slammed the door, and screeched out of the driveway.

I leaned back in my chair. Tony leaned back even further. We sat quietly smoking while the world rotated into darkness.

Bhangra Blow-Up
New York City
October 2004-August 2005

i. The Bed, March 2005

We never slept. It was early morning, and he was humping my leg. It was one of those Brooklyn apartments that had once been a home. Then some European immigrant had put up dry wall and turned it into a series of cramped apartments for non-European immigrants like us. You could end up getting a nice piece up front or a crappy piece in the back pantry next to a yard that was off-limits for all but the landlord. Ravi had gotten a piece of the front window and a broken archway over the bed.

"You remind me of Triumph," I said to him.

Triumph was The Insult Comic Dog, a puppet who interviewed politicians and celebrities. He was hot for a minute, but now he's just a distant thought. He's been shelved away in the place where old fads get shelved in human memory, the same warehouse as old loves and dead parts of us.

Triumph was a jerk to everyone. Still, he got a ton of interviews. Maybe because it was 2005, and every media channel was looking for some kind of distraction from what was really going on: a corrupt president and dead bodies filling up the ground.

I was looking for a distraction, too. "Triumph could really learn from you."

Ravi's eyes rolled up to the archway. "I take that as the

94

highest form of compliment, but it's more a meeting of equals. An exchange of notes."

ii. Bhangra Against Bush, October 2004

My first meeting with Ravi was by accident. We were returning from a night at Basement Bhangra. DJ Rekha had added a party to her regular night called Bhangra Against Bush. My sister and I went religiously. Some of the old crew from the desi political scene had even trickled back in.

There were plenty of sardars and black-pants girls. The sardars wore beards, turbans, button-down shirts and jeans. The black-pants girls wore stilettos, straightened their hair, and of course wore tight black pants. There was an endless stream of them coming from NYU. They never seemed to age, or perhaps the ones who started to immediately went on to graduate school or the wedding hall.

I felt terribly old. I'd spent my entire twenties trying to avoid getting married in a family that still practiced semi-forced arranged marriage. I was thirty and had won. The marriage proposals had slowed down to a trickle and eventually stopped. But as Bush said in sound bytes to justify the war: "Freedom comes at a cost."

I went home early that night. The subway platform was deserted. There was the sound of dripping water. It was just after midnight, the perfect time to head back to Brooklyn. The 2 train, my train, was going local. I could get on at Houston and not have to switch.

I was waiting for ten minutes when I heard the turnstile. It was Ravi. Just then, there were lights down the tunnel. The train.

"You're lucky," I said to him.

"No, no, no, not lucky." He had an accent I'd never heard before, one born from speaking English as a first language while growing up in Delhi.

"I guess you're thirty," I said.

He chuckled, and chuckled is the only word to describe it. "Why do you say that?"

"Because you're with me, going home early."

The train screeched to a halt. The doors opened, and we got in. He sat across from me and leaned forward with his big bulk. He was wearing a thin black coat and grey scarf. He looked like an overgrown Bengali child.

"Nice glasses," I said. They were square with a blue tint.

"I'm glad I spent extra in Delhi. I get a lot of compliments for them." The train lurched, but he caught himself before falling. "I hear you're a writer."

"I am."

"I am too."

"Really?" I thought he was a mathematician who did something with computers.

"I've been trying to get an agent," he said, "but I keep getting rejections. I was hoping to get in touch with Amitav Ghosh."

"Amitav?"

"You know him?"

"I just embarrassed myself with him once at a party. I do that all the time with famous people. I don't recognize them. I guess if you're famous that's considered rude."

Ravi started laughing, and I smiled. His laugh was like an orgasm. Then he said, "I have an even better story."

"Go ahead. I love stories."

And that's how it began.

Ravi made himself comfortable. I crossed my legs and sat back. The people in the rest of the subway ignored us.

"My father used to fly for business from Delhi to Bombay regularly. On one occasion, he was sitting next to a well-dressed man. Being quite friendly, my father tried to start up a conversation. 'So, do you live in Bombay?' The man looked at him for a few seconds and then said, 'Yes.' Not one to be daunted by a little resistance, my father continued, 'Do you work in Bombay?' The man fiddled with his drink and said in a barely tolerant voice, 'Yes, I work in Bombay.' 'Oh, are you in business?' 'No, I am not.' The man opened up a magazine, and my father got the hint and fiddled with his own drink. When they landed, the captain, stewardesses, and staff had all lined up to shake the hand of the man sitting next to my father. Just as he was stepping onto the ramp, my father heard the captain's excited voice, 'Thank you, thank you so much for flying with us, Mr. Bachchan.'"

"You're kidding me. How could your father not know he was sitting next to Amitabh Bachchan? Wasn't this India?"

"India in the Eighties, but my father didn't get out much."

"Disturbing." Little did I know, this obliviousness had been passed down from father to son. Outside, the green letters flashed. "This is my stop, Bergen."

"I'll get off."

"Don't you live on Carroll?"

"I can get off here."

He walked me to my door, and we said our good nights. I wonder sometimes if God looks down at those moments and laughs an evil laugh.

iii. The Election, November 2004

I didn't talk to Ravi again until the night of the second election Bush Junior took. Ravi was slumped on a bar couch in Brooklyn, his stomach hanging over his belt. He seemed out of place, a non-resident Indian in an American bar.

I'd gone to meet up with my sister, Safia, and her boyfriend, Qasim. Ravi was Qasim's roommate, and he followed the two of them wherever they went like a wind-up puppy dog. My sister and I were close, so I was starting to see Ravi more. He was beginning to register.

Everyone's eyes were glued to the TV as if it were the World Series. Suddenly voting had become important. People had even created sheets to keep count of the electoral votes. But everyone's balloon was about to pop. People knew. That's why they met in bars. Even though, if you asked me, bars were part of the problem.

I'd taken a break from the political scene, not for political reasons, but because I'd gone through rehab. Somehow, in New York City's South Asian activist scene, becoming sober was akin to changing political affiliations.

Ravi was sitting in a corner, apart from the crowd. He was going back to India in less than a year, so everything he observed was for the warehouse in his mind. He'd seal the box, label it "My Time in America," and draw stories from it now and then to entertain the literary crowd in Delhi. That was the night I fell into the box.

"You look tired," he said.

In the mirror above the bar, I could see my skin was a yellow-green. There were lines under my eyes. The beauty I stretched over myself like a thin Halloween mask had come off.

"A drink?"

"No, I'm going to an electoral vote counting party."

He shifted in his seat. "What's wrong with this one?"

I looked around. "Too white."

He couldn't disagree.

I walked the few blocks to my friend's apartment. All the bars and cafés were overflowing onto the street. There was noise all around until I turned down a quiet block. In front of the apartment, I saw a tree breaking through the sidewalk. The roots of the tree had lifted the concrete up.

I knew then Bush was going to steal the election. The war would continue, and eventually, with his help, the world as we knew it would be destroyed. Then the trees would break through. They'd take back the land we labeled the United States. It would be okay. The world would become the world it had been again.

iv. Inauguration, January 2005

Post-election, while the activists who'd fought to get Bush out of office were getting drunk, Ravi transferred himself from Qasim's and Safia's hips to mine. We were perfect for each other. I needed a substitute for drugs, and he needed a substitute for the entire subcontinent of India.

All the other women in the arty desi community started noticing Ravi as well. He managed to charm everyone with his stories and ability to pepper conversations with scatological jokes and mathematical theory.

All the women confided in my sister: "I have a crush on Ravi." His mojo was so intense, hardcore lesbians confessed, "I have a crush on Ravi." So when I approached my sister. I didn't have to finish. "Safia, I—"

"You have a crush on Ravi."

"How did you know?"

"Everyone has a crush on Ravi. Don't take it seriously."

"But—"

"Don't do it. He's a player."

"But I'm a player too."

"Not in the same way. And he's leaving." My sister had more common sense than I did. She always has. Later, when I had to leave New York, the city I loved, because every street corner, bar, sidewalk, and dog reminded me of him, she had the kindness to never say I told you so.

v. Skirts, February 2005

I would stare at Ravi's body when he wasn't looking. His butt sagged. He had long, heavy legs, a big belly, jowls, curly hair, and thick glasses, but he drove me crazy. I tried to explain it to my lawyer friend who saw a picture and was shocked by my obsession.

"This is the guy who's driving you mad with desire?"

I was embarrassed. "I don't know. Maybe I'm not in my right mind."

I wasn't. I was starting to unravel, the way I only did when I was looking for love in all the wrong places. I thought of Ravi all the time. I analyzed his every move. Was he attracted to me, or was he just lonely, looking for someone to fill in the gap of his last few months before returning home to India?

At the time in New York, there was an endless stream of desi art openings, dance parties, and film screenings. Ravi and I went to all of them, then met up for breakfast the next morning to analyze and dissect. Whether he was attracted to me, I didn't know, but I did know he was attracted to every beautiful woman he saw on the street.

"Whenever I see women in skirts, I just want to push them over and fuck them," he'd say, then quickly add, "but, of course, I'd never do that because it's wrong."

"How sensitive of you," I'd say, then light a cigarette. I'd started smoking again to deal with the constant sexual tension. I was so far gone, his awful comments didn't even make me blink.

Whether he wanted me, I didn't know, but I did wear skirts often when I was around him. It worked because I didn't fit into my jeans anymore. My body was changing, filling out right in front of my eyes, shifting from a malnourished drug addict's body to a full desi woman's.

On the phone with a friend, I confessed, "It's easy to be a feminist when you're twenty and beautiful. Then in your thirties, the lines around your eyes become like an Etch A Sketch, and you start to look like an aunty. I don't know. This whole thing with Ravi has turned me into another one of those insecure women lining up to buy expensive facial lotion."

My friends were astonished at the change in me and worried. "What's happening to you?" "Look at him. Look at you." "Why don't you call us anymore?" "You spend all your time with him. What's going on between you two?"

vi. Bhangra Blow-Up, March 2005

When Qasim's brother announced he was competing in Bhangra Blow-Up at Johns Hopkins, the four of us decided to take a road trip to Washington, D.C. Bhangra Blow-Up was a dance competition. It was like Circus of the Stars, except bhangra.

My sister had been dating Qasim for nine months now. He was a know-it-all computer geek, but at least he focused on Macs, unlike the other desi guys I knew who only did Windows and couldn't give me free advice for my MacBook.

Qasim's parents were as traditional as ours. They were coming to Bhangra Blow-Up so on the ride down we discussed strategy. It didn't matter if we were in our late twenties and early thirties. We were scared little kids when it came to our parents.

"I can't say I'm dating you, Safia," Qasim said. They were in the back seat.

"Fine. Why don't you say you're dating Razia?"

"No, I told them Ravi's dating Razia."

I turned to give her a look. I'd told her not to tell anyone about my crush.

My sister smiled. "Why don't you say we're both dating Ravi?"

Ravi, who was driving, laughed. "Fine with me."

It didn't help. Qasim's father was friendly, but his mother

barely said a word to us. After a very awkward introduction where she did her best to use her aunty powers to glare us to death, Qasim told us, "She called you Besharam."

"Besharam!" Safia and I both screeched.

"Well, she said Razia was Besharam. You're just her little sister who's coming along on a weekend date. But still, two girls away from home for a weekend with two men . . ." Qasim shook his head. He was getting so carried away with the drama, he was forgetting he was one of the men. I could see glimpses of the future uncle in him.

If Qasim's mother had been one of my personal aunties, it would have been disastrous. My parents would've found out immediately and disowned Safia or sent her to Pakistan to get married to a cousin. I'd already been down that road of disownment and didn't want to go there again. My family and I had finally made peace. We lived now in an uneasy truce following Clinton's "Don't Ask Don't Tell" policy.

Luckily, Qasim's mother was a few Pakistani social circles removed from ours, so we were safe. It was my first experience of aunty relativism, and Besharam became my nickname for the weekend. But Besharam, being without shame. Is that really such a bad thing?

vii. Bhangra Blow-Up, later that night

The dancers were college students from around the country. They had been training all year and were out to show their thing. Bhangra was supposed to be a traditional South Asian dance, but the moves they were doing were anything but— making pyramids like crazy Punjabi cheerleaders with facial hair.

Each team was more impressive than the next, jumping up onto each other's shoulders, spinning in the air, twisting, moving, and throwing their bodies until the crowd was going crazy. Their outfits matched their school colors and their mascots, chipmunks and bears, were dancing, too, dressed in lungis and salwars. I had no idea how the judges were ever going to decide.

I turned to Ravi. "It's so funny how these kids can rebel but still be part of the desi community. I don't understand."

He nodded and didn't say anything. I wasn't sure if he understood.

During half-time, an up-and-coming Bhangra singer performed. He came out in a white suit and bare feet. A voluptuous woman who looked like she was in her thirties accompanied him. She was all hoochied out. All the young girls looked like they had been starved in a closet for months, so it was wonderful to see this woman. I looked down at my own low-cut shirt. My newly expanding body was hard to keep contained in my clothes.

"Finally, someone who is representing my traditional costume," I said. "The Besharam."

"Look at those thighs." Ravi leaned so far forward in the tilted auditorium seats that I thought he'd topple over.

"Must you?" I asked.

"Maybe we can have a threesome?" He looked at me and raised his eyebrows.

I laughed. "We might have to wait in line." The skinny girls danced by. "Oh, are they still on stage?"

"Yes, I believe they were doing acrobatics a few steps away."

"I didn't notice."

And so it went. Ravi and I had fallen into the danger zone—the zone of friends who are attracted to each other just enough to be constantly in each other's company but not enough to rip off each other's clothes.

viii. Bhangra Blow-Up, later, later that night

NYU's team won for being the most traditional. The other teams limped home exhausted, some sustaining critical injuries. After the show was over, the masses poured out of the doors. The energy was explosive like the energy before a riot. Boys pulled away in cars, blasting Panjabi MC. Girls were in passenger seats, their straightened hair blowing from the tops of convertibles.

We could have stormed the White House right then, rushed across the lawn, and surprised everyone. We could've danced across the National Mall and torn out Lincoln's beard, protested the mandatory fingerprinting of South Asian and Arab men, protested the immigrant raids, the disappearances in the middle of the night.

Instead, the organizers had set up an after-party headlined by Raghav, our desi George Michael, our gorgeous crooner of R&B. It cost another hundred to go to the party, but for those of us who couldn't afford it, there were mini-parties scattered about where DJs would just play Raghav.

I wasn't familiar with D.C., but I had a feeling it wasn't always like this, with gangs of desis roaming the streets. As we were driving slowly through the crowds, trying not to hit anyone, Safia screamed, "Oh my God! It's Raghav!"

"Where? Where?" Ravi slammed on the brakes, afraid he

might have run Raghav over and would have to leave the country sooner than planned.

"Back there!" Safia pointed and we looked to see a stream of desis moving toward the spot as if they were magnetic filings.

We parked and ran, afraid if we didn't move fast enough the illusion would disappear.

"If I lose you in the crowd—" Ravi turned to me.

"If you lose me in the crowd, just look for the girl whose hair hasn't been straightened, and you'll find me."

"Good plan."

Raghav was standing on a catering table with a hand-held mic. He looked just like he did in the videos, a pretty boy with his hair softly gelled.

"How did you know it was Raghav?" I asked Safia.

She shrugged her shoulders. Raghav had that power over young girls. He was the ultimate magnetic force.

We couldn't get in through the front. It was too crowded, but for some reason there was a space cleared out right behind the table. The only thing which separated us from Raghav was a row of fake bushes and his bodyguards.

All along the table there was a mass of gorgeous desi girls, each one more beautiful than the next. Their hair gleamed under the streetlights. They reached out their arms to touch Raghav, throw flowers. From where we were standing, we could see the naked hunger in their faces. Raghav would move to the right, and the girls would sway to the right. He'd move to the left, and the girls would sway to the left. He wouldn't give one girl all of himself but would give each a little bit, just enough so she'd want more.

Ravi turned to one of the bodyguards. "Hello."

The guards looked at him through narrow eyes, but Ravi's charm applied to men as well. He gave them one of his goofy grins, and they softened. "What's going on here?" he asked.

"Shooting." The guards crossed their arms until their muscles bulged.

"Shooting?"

"Shooting at the club."

It turned out the desi party promoters had skimped on getting metal detectors, and no one had patted the boys down. The energy *had* exploded, and when the shooting began, Raghav was whisked away. Just like real royalty.

We'd caught the tail end of the impromptu concert. Raghav finished, threw kisses, and bowed. His bodyguards moved aside the potted plants to make a walkway, and suddenly we were face to face. Raghav looked surprised, as if he couldn't believe he was such a star himself.

Ravi reached out and patted him on the shoulder. "Good show, man."

Raghav smiled a shy smile, nodded, then disappeared into the night.

Ravi and I went to party after party, long after my sister and Qasim had left because they were tired. As we were dancing, Ravi leaned in and whispered in my ear, "Who's thirty now?"

ix. Exotification

We got home a little bit before dawn. Ravi went to the bathroom to change, and I quickly did the same, then started laying out the sleeping bags on the floor of our friend's living room.

A few minutes later, he came to bed wearing salwar kameez.

I sat up. "Wow."

"What?"

"Nothing." I felt ridiculous saying it. "You just look good in salwar kameez."

He put his hands on his hefty hips and pouted. "Are you exotifying me?"

I looked down. I was. "No."

"Yes! You're exotifying me." He started laughing.

"But how can I be exotifying you if it's my own culture?"

He raised his eyebrows. "It's not your culture."

I stopped. How could I argue with him? "It's just that I haven't seen any man wearing that to bed but my father and uncles."

Ravi got into the sleeping bag and shifted around until he got comfortable. "Oh, so this is Oedipal?"

I got into my bag, too. "Not Oedipal. It's Electra. Oedipal is for a boy being into his mother."

"Right, Electra."

Whatever it was, I was hopelessly turned on.

Ravi zippered up his sleeping bag, and I curled into mine. A few minutes later, he was snoring softly, but I couldn't sleep. It wasn't lost on me that Ravi was a present day version of what my father and uncles had been. They had paved the way, knocking their foreheads against the concrete of New York City, working in stores, factories, and low-level labs. They made room for the likes of Ravi so his kind could come like big spoiled children and leave the same.

Ravi let out a snort. I turned. His mouth was slightly open and his face dark in the light filtering in through the window. If I had followed the way set out for me by my family, I would have been going to bed with a man who wore salwar kameez every night. Maybe I had made some bad choices in my life. But it was ridiculous to think this way. I could only be the person I had been born to become.

x. Tom Waits, the next day

There were groans from the backseat while Waits growled, "Temptation, temptation . . ."

"No more, no more Tom Waits!" It was Qasim loudly whining.

"Yeah," my sister said. "Mixed CDs are supposed to be a mix, not just Tom Waits." They laughed, then high-fived each other like evil little kids.

We were on our way back from D.C., and all their complaining was annoying me. I turned the volume up in the rental car.

"You know they use music to torture Muslim men," Qasim said. "They blast heavy metal at detainees until they lose their minds."

My stomach twisted. "Okay, okay." I turned the volume down. He had made his point.

Ravi turned around. "Kids. Settle down. Who needs a bathroom break?"

"We want ice cream!" Qasim and Safia yelled.

We pulled over at the next rest stop and while they went to the bathroom, Ravi and I walked to a patch of grass that was between one highway and the next. The cars hurtled past us. The sky itself was beginning to show streaks of color like bleeding roadkill.

"Ah, the liminal space," Ravi murmured.

"Liminal space?"

"Yes." He stretched out his legs and groaned like a middle-aged man.

"Are you going to explain?"

"Liminal spaces. Let me see if I can quote Turner." Ravi had a way of talking sometimes that was textbook perfect, but unlike the ones he memorized, he made everything seem something worth knowing. "'A place where boundaries dissolve. Where we stand on the threshold, getting ourselves ready to move across the limits of what we were into what we are to be.'"

"Hmph. Moving across what we are to be." I looked at the uncut grass. It waved frantically every time a car sped by. I looked at Ravi. He was sweating slightly from the short walk across the highway. God, I was so hot for him.

Ravi wasn't done. "It represents a period of ambiguity, of marginal and transitional states, a possibility for cultural hybridity. In the urban setting, a place such as this. In the cultural sense, an event such as Bhangra Blow-Up. In the geographic, these rest stops and the impossibility of taking a shit in any one of them."

I laughed. Safia and Qasim were crossing the highway to join us.

Ravi leaned in and whispered, "It felt strange not sleeping next to you last night."

I looked at him, shocked. After months of wondering if he was attracted to me, he had just given me the green light.

xi. Home Sweet Home, later that night

We got back to New York City late. It was pouring. The brown-stones were wet, dark figures in the night. The streets were shining black with rain. We gathered our bags from the car, along with all the junk we had accumulated over the weekend, then squeezed into the lobby.

A smell of wet funk came from the apartment. "Home, sweet home," Safia said.

We were exhausted. Safia and Qasim went to one bedroom, and Ravi went to his. I was left standing in the living room by myself. The sofa was covered with books on mathematics. Buried underneath was a well-worn copy of *People* magazine. I didn't want to know why it was well-worn. I decided I didn't want to sleep on the dirty sofa another night.

Safia came in with blankets, a sheet, and a pillow.

"I'm going to do it, Safia. I'm going to ask him if I can sleep in his bed," I said.

She clenched her jaw the way she always did when I said something really, really stupid. "Don't."

"But he told me he wanted to sleep with me."

She seemed skeptical. "He did?"

"Don't sound so surprised."

"I don't agree with it," she said, but I didn't turn around to hear what else she had to say.

I went into Ravi's bedroom where we had spent so much time as friends. I stood in front of his bed and looked at him.

"Did I miss my chance to sleep with you?"

"No." He shook his head and pulled me into the bed.

And just like that our friendship ended.

xii. Plastic Glass, the next morning

The next morning, his body was warm, soft. I moved to get up.

"Wait," he said. "Stay. I've got to make the most of this. My purchase of a Queen-size mattress is finally paying off."

I laughed and pulled close to him, but eventually we had to get up. Neither of us had the money to pay for an extra day for the rental. We had been so broke, we had gotten the car from Jersey City.

As we surfaced from the Holland Tunnel, he turned to me. "Last night was amazing."

I smiled. Even Jersey seemed beautiful then in the light.

We took the PATH train back. It slid out and under the Hudson. As we drew closer to the city, everything grew dark. We were coming through a valley it seemed, a demolition site. There were bolts in the concrete the size of cars.

I looked out the window. "Where are we?"

Ravi got up. "Razia, I think we just entered Ground Zero."

"Oh no, no, no." I looked to see if there was an exit. I'd said I'd never come here. This place whose destruction had changed the city I loved into a minefield, changed the entire country into a war machine.

"It was an accident," Ravi said. For a second, I didn't know what he meant.

We pressed our faces against the plastic glass.

xiii. Orange Juice, April 2005

And just like that we became lovers. His eyelashes fallen all over the pillow, the laughter squeezed out of us, a window which was finally next to a tree. At night, Ravi read to me from Saroyan's *The Poor and Burning Arab*. Then we'd turn out the lights to go to sleep, but we never did.

One afternoon, I left work and stood under the strange piece of clockwork in Union Square. The orange numbers flashed above me. I called Ravi.

He sounded terrible.

"Are you sick?"

He moaned.

"Do you want me to come over, bring you some orange juice?"

"No. Don't come over." He was miserable and stuffy.

"Are you afraid I'm going to get sick?"

"No. I know how hardy you Pathans are. I just don't want to be the pathetic guy who needs his girlfriend to come over when he's got a cold."

He had never called me his girlfriend before. I smiled. "I wasn't thinking of it that way. I was thinking of how easy it would be to take advantage of you in your weakened state."

He laughed. "In that case, come on over."

I went down into the subway, full of light.

xiv. [17, 13, 2 ...]

We were in his bed, my new home away from home, when Ravi asked from out of nowhere, "How many people have you slept with?"

I looked at him. "Do you really want to know?"

"Yes."

"Well . . ." I got up and pulled the hair out of my face, some of it from my mouth. "I don't really know how to answer. Because with men it means penetration, but with women it could be oral sex, but then that would make it oral sex with men, and the numbers would quadruple. I guess I could count the women I've slept with since I got my dildo, but it wouldn't be fair because I only just bought my dildo a few years ago, so then I'd have to backdate to all the women I might have used a dildo on if I had a dildo to use. This brings us purely into the theoretical, or as they say, imaginary numbers. It's like a series in brackets: 17, 13, 2. . . . The solution for the pattern would be: n times parentheses n minus one over 2005 minus the year I bought my dildo times—"

"Okay, okay, stop." He was laughing.

"What about you?" I asked.

He looked a little embarrassed. "You're number two."

"Two as in?"

"Two as in two, the real number."

"You only slept with one person before me? Wow." I laid back and tried to absorb it. "Your white girlfriend?"

"Yes, but I slept with her many, many times in the course of a year and a half."

I laughed. "No wonder you wanted to marry her."

He sighed. "I don't think it would have been a good marriage for her."

"Why?"

Ravi pulled the sheets away and sat up. He put his glasses back on. "On my last visit, I was telling her about my research on algorithms, and she turned to me and said she had faked all her orgasms." He looked at me through the thick frames of his glasses, "Do you?"

I was wearing nothing more than a tank top. I pulled it down a little bit. "I'm a very selfish and self-centered person, Ravi. Why would I fake them? There'd be nothing in it for me." He didn't seem to believe me and continued to look distressed. "Ravi, if I was going fake them, wouldn't I have already?"

The logic of that statement made sense, and he relaxed. It was true. Although God had blessed me with an orgasmic body, for some reason with Ravi, it didn't always happen. He'd feel bad, and I'd say it was all right. Then we'd stay up all night making jokes.

I used to ask my friends, "Why do you sleep with someone who doesn't get you off?" I had to eat my own self-righteous words after I met Ravi. I knew the answer now.

xv. The Phone Call

"I found the perfect man for you, Razia. He's not religious. He's bald, and he eats pork." It was ten o'clock in the morning, and my older orthodox cousin was calling to save me from old maidenhood. Ravi and I were still in bed. I put my finger to my lips so he wouldn't say anything.

"What? Tamina, don't call me so early in the morning."

"Okay. I'll call you later."

"No. Don't—" but she had already hung up.

I turned to Ravi and filled him in. "Are these the marriage proposals I'm going to be getting from now on?"

He tried to suppress his laughter.

"What?"

"It's just for years you got proposals from the men who drove the BMWs, and now you're getting offers from the men who fill them up."

I lit a cigarette and tried to sit so I didn't choke on the smoke. "Okay, that is messed up on so many levels, I can't even go there right now."

The truth was I deflected marriage proposals every Monday and Wednesday ever since I'd gotten a job in Queens teaching teachers how to teach poetry. One of the perks was that I got picked up at my apartment in Brooklyn and taken to Queens in a Sky Cab limo.

The company was owned by desis, run by desis, and the cars were driven by desis. I realized I had to develop an alternate life story for the drivers just to make my life easier.

The first time I got in the minivan, the driver asked me to sit in the front. The whole back was empty. A lifetime of being around molesting uncles put me on guard, but just like the little girl who couldn't say no to someone older, I did.

As soon as I got in, the third degree started. "Desi?"

I hesitated. I knew where this would go if I told the truth. I readied myself. "Yes."

A big grin. "Married?"

"No-ot yet," I said, then quickly added, "but I'm engaged to my cousin in Pakistan."

"Mother's side or father's side?"

"Father's."

"Yes, father's is always best."

I nodded, even though my father's side was much crazier ever since they'd gotten displaced by the Tarbela Dam.

"Studying?"

"Yes."

"What?"

"Dentistry." It was the first thing that came to my mind.

I smiled and hoped he wouldn't ask why my teeth were crooked, but then I remembered desi dentists always had terrible teeth.

"Dentistry, a good profession."

"Is it?" It's totally sick and gross, I thought.

"I left Punjab seven years ago," he said to me, keeping his eyes on the road. "I haven't seen my children since. My son was two when I left. He's nine now." His loneliness made me uncomfortable. "When I first came here, I couldn't believe the clothes on the ladies. In India, I looked at girls, but here my eyes came out of my head when I saw these American ladies showing everything. And the Spanish, Voh to nangey hain. I got used to it, but I don't like when I see our girls doing the same thing." He looked at my covered legs. "You are a very good girl." I hadn't been called a good girl since puberty.

Somehow the man arranged to be my driver. So on every ride after, I would slowly build on my story. I knew how to make biryani. I had five brothers. My fiancé was studying computers, but of course, he'd have to do it all over again at The Chubb Institute when he got here (those racist Americans).

For those weeks, the cab driver got to know me, well, not me, but the fake me. I got to know her, too, a girl I would have been in another life.

Who knows? Maybe he was lying to me, too.

xvi. The Alley

Something strange started happening with Ravi. The more intimate we became, the more ashamed I felt to be seen with him in public. I told him I didn't want anyone to know. I knew how women wanted him and felt strange being the one he was with. Plus, I had an irrational fear of being seen with a man around other desis. It came from years of growing up in Corona's Muslim community. Even though the desis I hung out with were queer, progressive, and into drugs and polyamory, it still felt like my neighborhood where everyone was watching.

We were at a party at the White Rabbit. I felt awkward dancing with Ravi, so I danced with everyone but him. Ravi sat on a sofa by himself.

Eventually, he got up to leave. "Razia, can I see you outside?" He seemed frustrated and strange.

"Okay." We walked into the Lower East Side night.

When we left the bar, the desi girls who were smoking gave us knowing looks.

"I'm sorry. I gave us away by bringing you out here."

"It's okay. What is it?" He pulled me around the corner onto Allen Street.

It was an alleyway. He pushed me back against the wall in the corner between a garbage dumpster and the entrance of the F train. I was wearing a denim miniskirt and black boots. He started to kiss me and put his hand under my shirt. Years of living in Delhi, where girls would never let him go below the belt, made Ravi an expert on above the belt. In short, he was an amazing kisser. Plus, there is nothing like making out on a hot spring night in an alley next to a dumpster.

He stopped and pulled away.

"What is it?" I asked again.

"Amina asked me out."

I pulled back, which was hard to do because there was a dirty brick wall behind me. I looked at him. "What do you want to do?"

"I don't know." That wasn't the right answer. "I wish I could bring you home with me."

"You know I can't go home with you tonight." My friend was visiting from out of town.

He paused, then sighed, "I'd like to see other women before I go."

I felt my stomach plunge. I didn't understand how he could say he wanted me to come home with him and to see other women in the same breath.

xvii. Aishwarya Rai

My friends tried to comfort me. "It doesn't matter how ugly these Indian men are. They all think they can get Aishwarya Rai."

"Because they can," I said. "Arranged marriage, remember? All they have to do is point their fat fingers at a woman and she's his."

xviii. The Bulgarian Disco, May 2005

The Bulgarian Disco was the new hot spot. Well, it was the old hot spot for Bulgarians in New York, but the rest of us had just found out. Ravi and I were doing what white people did to our desi spaces. We were outsiders trying to get a piece of ethnic European action.

At the door, a very small man yelled out, "Oh no! Pakistanis!" Ravi noticeably winced. But the very small man was a co-worker of mine.

"Hey there," I said before I lost him in the crowd.

We pushed up and past the bodies filling the stairs off Canal Street all the way up to the second floor where there were even more bodies. Luckily, Eastern Europeans are thin. Otherwise, it would have been impossible to have so many in such a small room.

Ravi had a funny look on his face. After the night at the White Rabbit, we had talked about seeing other people. I'd told Ravi I'd rather be friends than do something open. I'd had enough of open relationships. He told me he'd rather date me than go back to being friends.

Still, I knew the Eastern European women were turning him on. He tried to focus on dancing with me. I tried to focus on dancing with him, but my heart was in my stomach. Ever since the conversation, it felt off. Slowly, the easy banter, the flirting, the jokes, the laughter had been replaced by a constant sense of unease and anxiety. The sex had become forced. Ravi

would get hard, then soft. He'd get hard again, then soft. My
body would close down. Completely close up.

xix. Torture

"Hey, come over here," he said.

I was slowly pulling off my stockings and my boots. Ravi was sitting on a chair by the window. I went and sat in his lap. I was tiny, tiny compared to him. He was naked, looking out onto the street, and smoking a cigarette. We had just returned from The Bulgarian Disco and tried to have sex, but Ravi couldn't get hard.

He put out his cigarette. "What do you think of having one of those Bulgarian women over for a threesome?"

I became ice cold. The words that came out of my mouth were cut glass on top of a fence. "Ravi, if you want to fuck a white woman before you leave for India, go ahead."

He looked at me through dark eyes and then lit another cigarette. "I guess I'm just not as attracted to you as I thought."

The immediate burn took my breath away. I stood up. It was another hot spring night and my skin peeled off his lap. I leaned against the window, lit a cigarette, and looked out. My hands were shaking until my body filled up with smoke. My lungs were turning into the tar streets outside, and like the streets, they were empty.

"Men always blame women for their own bullshit." I didn't look at him when I said it.

"Yes, this is true," he agreed and hung his head. "I'm sorry." The other uncircumcised head hung down as well.

But the burn was made, as if he had taken his cigarette and

held it to my skin. Lit the flame right there. Every moment I spent with Ravi, I was degrading myself, but the moments with him were so few, I felt I couldn't tear myself away.

xx. Spine like a Jellyfish, June 2005

Nothing was ever the same. We tried to meet up and talk, but the bitterness and hurt kept the words from coming out the way I needed them to. There weren't any words to bring our friendship back. Ravi was leaving at the end of July, so all I had to do, I thought, was wait.

But the month passed slow, and I tossed and turned on my old mattress, crying uncontrollably, feeling as if a part of myself had been blasted out. Every block of my neighborhood, every bar, club, theater reminded me of him. I thought I'd lost my city before, but this was the real thing.

My sister called, and when she heard I was in a state, she came by. She walked into my bedroom, stepping between the clothes and papers which were strewn everywhere.

"You don't want to talk to him?"

"Who? Ravi? No."

"He didn't date Amina. He's in bed depressed, waiting to leave."

I shrugged. It didn't really help me what Ravi was or wasn't doing.

xxi. Balls the Size of a Bull's, July 2005

I was running out the door, heading to a second shift of work when I heard the phone ring. We didn't have caller ID and without thinking, I picked it up.

"Hello, Razia?" It was Ravi. My mouth went into my gut. I didn't say anything. "Razia, I'm leaving next Friday."

"I know."

"Would you, I was wondering if you'd . . ." he cleared his throat, "spend the last night with me."

That was Ravi, balls the size of a bull's and just as useless.

I paused and breathed into the space.

My friends were furious. But how could I explain? I knew if he left and I didn't see him, he'd leave with all my chances of taking back my dignity.

xxii. Temptation

Ten years in this country and Ravi was sitting in a chair eating a banana and freaking out. It was an incredibly hot July night, the kind of night that had already slipped into August. The air was wet. I sat on the floor taking CDs out of their cases and putting them into the sleeves of a CD album.

"Hey, how did you end up with the Tom Waits road trip CD?"

He smiled. "Don't tell Safia and Qasim, but I play it all the time."

I looked down so he wouldn't see I was about to cry. We had an unspoken pact to not say anything of what had happened in the spring. There just wasn't time. I had left enough places to know I was already a shadow while he was a projection of himself in the future.

"There is only that one moment," he sighed from his arm-chair, "when the dean shakes your hand and gives you your diploma when you are fully a Doc. Before that you're ABD, for the rest of your life, a Postdoc."

I laughed then had an inspiration. "Ravi. You know how you always wanted to push beautiful women over and pull up their skirts?"

"Yes?" He was temporarily distracted from his academic malaise.

"Well, I'm wearing a skirt."

His eyes grew wide.

I took the banana from his hands and led him to the bed. This time I was ready for all his hang-ups. I remembered all the moments he'd gotten soft, and one second before it was about to happen, I'd switch up. I played his body like a person played an out-of-tune piano, moving my fingers around and around until I realized it wasn't out of tune at all. I'd just been playing it all wrong.

xxiii. To Do

While Ravi was in the shower, I picked up the handwritten "To Do" list off the floor. I'd made it for him earlier and insisted there should be boxes next to each item.

"There's so much more satisfaction that way. See? You do a thing, then check it off."

I looked at the list:

☐ Return library books
☐ Take packages to post office
☐ Buy CD album
☐ Pack CDs . . .

I put:

☐ Hot sex with Razia

Made a box and checked it off.

xxiv. Going Home

The cab pulled up in front. I was sitting on the stoop, smoking a cigarette. It was my job to watch the suitcases.

The driver was desi, and when he found out Ravi was going back to India for good, he was impressed. Ravi was doing what all our fathers, uncles, and desi cab drivers said they would do one day. He was going home.

I smiled to myself a dark smile. The joke was on me. I'd never been competing with the women in New York. I'd been competing with Mother India.

"You can have him, Mother India," I said.

Safia was coming out with another suitcase. "Who're you talking to?"

"Mother India."

She raised her eyebrows but didn't say anything.

I helped Ravi lift one of the larger suitcases into the trunk. The handle snapped off. He started laughing, and Safia and I looked at each other. Maybe he was losing it.

In between giggles, Ravi managed to say, "The man on Canal Street said this would be the perfect suitcase if I was planning on not coming back. He was telling the truth."

xxv. The Mattress, August 2005

As a parting gift, like the kind they give contestants to make their public humiliation worth it, Ravi gave me his Queen-size mattress.

"It's barely been used," he said.

I couldn't help but laugh. Even though every New Age book would have told me to burn that shit, my writer's budget combined with the back problems I was developing from my own terrible mattress made the acceptance necessary.

Qasim brought it over a few weeks after Ravi left, but it was so big it got stuck on the second floor. After pushing and pushing, we gave up and just left it there.

Then one night, I was having dinner with some butch friends I hadn't seen in a few months. I told them about the mattress and the whole disastrous story of me and Ravi. In true butch fashion, they offered to come over and get the mattress upstairs.

"You've been through enough," one of them said.

"I have a tool kit in the back of my car," the other said. "We can saw off any parts that don't fit."

They did just that. They sawed off one corner and the mattress slid upstairs like a fish rushing upstream to get laid. That night in Ravi's bed, for the first time in months, I slept. I dreamt of water while somewhere across the Gulf, a hurricane rose to come across the land.

G-TV (Episode Two)
New Rochelle, New York
May 2005

"Razeeah, let me ask you a question. Honesty, when it's not honest, is that bad?"

We were making drinks in the kitchen, some kind of berry-blast malt and apple Bacardi. I was sitting, enjoying the afternoon sun and Tony. I hadn't seen him as much since I'd moved to Brooklyn, but things weren't going so well, and I needed the kind of advice only Tony could give.

I was hoping he'd be home alone, but Stupid Joe was there, too, looking like he'd just stepped off the glossy page of a magazine. Poor Stupid Joe, looking good was the only thing he had going. I was breaking my sobriety pledge, but it was all I could do to keep myself together after what had happened with Ravi. Tony handed me my drink. It was pink and full of ice. These guys, they loved their frou-frou drinks. I took a long sip, looked out the window, what used to be my kitchen window, and smiled.

After I moved out, Tony and Benny had fixed my old place up so Tony and his new girlfriend, Gina, could move in, but everything from the window looked the same: the squares of quiet lawn, old Johnny in his shorts, young Johnny's widowed grandmother all in black: her skirt, sweater, headscarf.

I was at the Russo's because I wanted to hide from what was going on with me. I was at the Russo's because I wanted to get drunk in the afternoon where no one would judge me. I was at the Russo's because when I was feeling this horrible, Tony was the only one who could cheer me up.

And the cheering up began right away.

"Honesty—when it's not honest," I said. "Let me think

about that." I took another long sip. God, it tasted good. "I always thought honest was the root word for honesty, but maybe the root word is something else like nest or sty."

Joe was a little slow, but Tony started laughing. And it hit me. He'd missed me.

"Razeeah, damn you, maybe you can give me some advice. Gina—"

"Tony, what did you do?"

He lit a cigarette even though Gina's rule was no smoking in the house.

"It's not what you think, Razeeah. I didn't do anything bad, like cheat on her. Hey, can you open the window?"

I turned around and started pulling. It still got stuck the way it used to. I had to throw my weight against it to get it to open. "That's good," I said, relieved. Even though I missed his old girlfriend, Maria, Gina was the one who knew how to save Tony from himself.

"But," Joe broke in, "it's not cheating if you're not engaged."

I snorted up my Bacardi, and Tony just shook his head. We looked at Joe like he was an idiot, but I was curious about his reasoning. Sometimes it was fun to see how Joe thought.

"Joe, what the hell are you talking about?"

"I'm just saying, if you're not engaged to a girl, it's not cheating."

"Joe, that's so stupid. If Gina slept with anyone else, I'd be pissed."

Joe looked at us like we were the ones who were hopeless. "Look, whoever you're with, eventually you're going to break up with them, then you're going to say I'm glad I fucked those other girls when I had the chance."

"But Joe," I said, trying not to laugh, "maybe if you hadn't fucked those other girls, your relationship would have lasted."

"I don't care." He was defensive now because he knew I was laughing at him. "You can sleep around if you don't have a ring."

"You know Joe," I said, "I just broke up with this Indian guy because he wanted to have sex with other people." Tony looked at me. "Tony, can you give me a cigarette?" He did, and I could see from his mouth he was getting angry at this guy he'd never met. "Thanks Tony." I lit the cigarette and took a drag before continuing, "I've already done the open-relationship thing. I don't want to do it again."

Joe looked at me with new interest. "You were in an open relationship?" I knew what was going through his mind, and I didn't know if I liked it.

"For three years," I said. I looked back at Tony, and for a moment it passed between us, those three years of nights when he had listened to the ups and downs of my ridiculous love life.

"Yeah, but that's why I want monogamy now. I want to be with someone who just wants to be with me." Even as I said it, it seemed impossible, like something I'd never have.

Joe shook his head, and I could tell he wanted to help. "Razeeah, you're living in the wrong place for that. You live in the city where everyone's hot. Whenever I go to the city, everywhere I look I see a girl I want to fuck. You've got to live in the suburbs or something if you want monogamy."

I looked at Tony, and he shrugged. If we listened to Joe too much, he started to make sense.

"Anyway," I said. I put the lit cigarette in the ashtray and got up to make another drink. I felt naked all of a sudden. "Tony what were you talking about? Gina?"

The kitchen was small. Joe was leaning against the stove, and he moved aside to let me get to where the bottles were.

Tony was quiet at first. He watched me. But I didn't want

them to feel sorry for me. "So?" I said.

"Razeeah, I'm sorry. If you want me to—"

"What? Take care of him? No, that's okay. He's leaving the country. But tell me what happened with Gina before she gets home."

"Shit Razeeah. You have to act like you don't know anything when you see her."

I raised the drink to my heart. "I promise." I was getting drunk.

"Well, Gina had a procedure last week."

"Procedure? What do you mean a procedure?" I sat back down and picked up my cigarette.

"Liposuction."

"What?" I thought of how skinny Gina was. "Where on her body did they find fat?"

"I know Razeeah. I tried to talk her out of it, but you know Gina, she does her own thing. But that's not the problem. See, her doctor prescribed her some pain meds . . ." Now I knew where this was going. "And we had the best fucking time last weekend. We were running around the mall, cracked out of our minds. We even went to the Discovery Store. Hey Razeeah, have you ever heard of tree hugging? I was reading in this energy book it's a great way to get grounded." He took a long drag of his cigarette. "Razeeah, have you ever hugged a tree?"

I laughed, and the air around me was light again. "I've hugged a tree or two in my time."

Joe looked back and forth between us like we'd lost our minds. "What do you mean, you hugged a tree? Naked?"

Tony and I both started cracking up.

"Joe, you idiot, you're not supposed to be getting off on the tree. You're just supposed to be hugging it." We shook our heads. Joe never quite got it. Tony continued, "So I thought, you know, we had such a good time. I told Gina to call her doctor and say she was still in pain so he could prescribe some more pills. But the doctor's secretary told Gina if she was still in pain, she needed to come in for a follow-up."

I shook my head. "Tony, you can't just get pain meds like that. They're a controlled substance."

"I know. I forgot. Of course." He smiled. "You're not supposed to be in more pain a week later."

We both started laughing. It really wasn't funny, but then again, it was. Through the window I could hear old Johnny mowing his lawn. The kitchen was full of sun, and I realized I loved these guys, my life, New Rochelle.

But I tried to think of Gina. "Tony, I'd be mad too. What's Gina gonna do?"

"I don't know, but she's really mad at me. Razeeah, why the hell do doctors have to make you feel like such a crackhead for wanting to have some fun?"

I hid my smile by taking a long drink. "Yeah, don't they know you're already stressed? Why else would you need to snort pain meds?"

"Razeeah!" He slapped his hand on the counter. "That's what I'm saying. I mean, so I like popping pills. If it makes me a drug addict, is that really so bad?"

Joe and I looked at each other. Actually, we all did think it was bad the way Tony was with pills.

"But now my girl's mad at me. She called me up and said I was a crackhead, that I made her lie, and she never lies, and I put her in a bad situation."

"Did you say sorry?"

"Razeeah, of course. For a whole hour and a half on the phone today I was apologizing."

Joe nodded his head. "He did. For a whole hour and a half

on the phone."

"But she's still pissed." Tony ground his cigarette out in the sink and then ran water over the spot of dark ash. "See, my girl and I are different. She's all about keeping it real and being honest. Me? I have no problem with telling a lie to save my ass."

I shook my head. "Tony, you're crazy."

"But damn, Razeeah, I don't want her to be mad. What should I do?"

He looked at me, and I could tell he really did feel bad.

"You've got to apologize again after she's cooled down."

"Yeah, but Razeeah," Joe was serious now, "let me ask you something. With girls, when should you say sorry? If you fuck up and you say sorry, and then you say sorry again later, your girl gets all mad. She looks at you like, 'Why're you bringing this up again?'"

Tony looked at me. Every so often, they asked me things they couldn't ask their girlfriends.

I sat up straight and lit another cigarette. I liked being the expert. "Well, the first sorry is the knee-jerk sorry, and your girl knows it. She knows you haven't even thought about what you did or processed it. You're just saying sorry to cover your ass. Who is going to believe that?"

Tony started cracking up. "Razeeah! You're the best! Knee-jerk sorry. It is!"

I smiled, but inside I was thinking of how Ravi had apologized and apologized for making me feel like shit and how it had meant nothing to me. I knew it had just been a knee-jerk sorry.

"So," Joe said, and I could see his perfectly-shaped eyebrows come together on his head, "should you not even apologize in the beginning?"

Tony and I both started laughing. I almost couldn't stop. Yes, coming here was the best thing I could've done.

"Come on Joe," I said. "Let's go outside. Tony, call Gina and say sorry like you mean it."

Tony touched my arm. "Razeeah, you really are the best. You should tell this guy to go fuck himself."

I smiled. "I don't think he has any other choice."

When Joe and I got out on the porch, Valerio was sitting on the steps smoking. "Hey Razeeah!" I sat down next to him. His shirt was dirty and so were his hands. I could see he was only slightly drunk today. But still I felt worried. He seemed to have aged ten years since I had moved out.

"Razeeah, look who's here." He pointed as if Joe was invisible to me. "It's Joe. Look, he's a good-looking guy. Why don't you go out with him?"

I smiled. Valerio was always trying to get me to go out with one of the neighborhood boys.

Joe looked at me, and I was surprised he looked hopeful. I laughed. "He is Valerio, but I've already got boy problems."

Valerio threw his cigarette over the porch into the bushes. "Ah. Razeeah, you know what I think. Love, God, George Bush. It's all shit!"

I smiled, took a drag off my cigarette and threw it half-lit into the bushes after him. "I know, Valerio. It is."

Abandoned Bread Truck
Corona, Queens
January 1985

Every few weeks, and really it could have been less, an abandoned car showed up outside our dining room window. The car would be left there sometime on a Saturday night, whole for just a moment before it would start to decay. Every morning after that, pieces would go missing. The tires would be the first to vanish. Then the windows would be shattered and the insides gutted. Finally, the engine lid would pop open and pieces would disappear. Then, as suddenly as the car had come, it would be gone. Its space wouldn't be empty for long before another car would show up to take its place.

On winter mornings, I would sit on the radiator by the window. Some days, it was the only way to stay warm. I would see the abandoned cars and imagine I was living in the desert, or the high distant plain, walking past the same dead animal, wolf, laid to rest on the sand and in the heat. I'd watch the way pieces of it would disappear, stripped by secret claws and beaks. Pieces would always disappear while I was asleep.

Then there was one day, a bitter January morning, when a bread truck delivering fresh Italian bread, stalled right outside of our house. The truck driver was a big Italian. He got out and cursed and kicked the truck. His curses made smoke in the air. He walked off to find a pay phone, but there was no working pay phone anywhere in Corona. He walked around the corner and disappeared.

It was a snow day, and already children were coming outside to make snow angels and pretend they were skating on patches of ice. They came out in their boots and their cheap coats from Alexander's. It was Julio and his friends who noticed the abandoned bread truck first. There was always a group of boys who moved around Julio like wobbly planets.

I leaned against the window and watched them. They circled the truck, a child they were ready to gang up on. Julio jumped up to the cab and tried to pull open the door, but it was locked. His friends threw snowballs as if they were handballs. The white on white hit the metal and bounced off the truck. But soon even they got bored with that and wandered off to make trouble somewhere else.

Across the street in the buildings, I began to see faces in the windows: the three old Italian ladies who always wore black, the young Dominican mothers of the kids in my school holding baby brothers and sisters on their hips. The bread truck had made the mistake of stalling on the street where all the abandoned cars were left. Everyone was watching to see what would happen.

The old Italian ladies were the first to disappear from their windows. As if they had been given a signal, they all vanished from their different apartments. They showed up again, on the snow, like black crows on ice. I saw them creep up to the back of the truck. I ran to tell my mother. She was in the kitchen scrubbing the counters with Mr. Clean.

"Ammi, something's happening." By the time my mother washed her hands and came back with me to the dining room window, there was a mob on the street.

Julio had come back with his father and a crowbar. His father looked around for the driver, and when he saw no one, he popped open the back like he was opening a can of soda, then jumped into the truck. He was gone for a few minutes. We all waited, not knowing what to do. When he came out, his arms were full of loaves of bread. He threw an armful to Julio who ran home with it.

Slowly, other people started coming to the back of the truck. The old Italian ladies were at the head, but behind them was the Korean grandmother, the young Dominican mothers, and other kids from my school. Some of them waited for Julio's father to throw them bread. Others jumped in themselves and grabbed armfuls of Italian bread with or without seeds, rolls and whole loaves. They ran home hugging the fresh bread to their chests.

I looked up at my mother, waiting for her to say something about the people in our neighborhood, but instead she said, "Put on your coat."

"Kya?" I said, afraid I would get in trouble if I had misheard. This was the same mother who made me walk back to the bodega on the corner to give back even five cents any time they gave me too much change.

She said again, "Put on your coat and get some bread."

When I got outside, it felt like someone had thrown a block party in the middle of the winter street. I had never seen my neighbors smiling at each other this way. I walked to the back of the truck, feeling cold in my thin coat.

But the ice of January was nothing when Julio's father put a loaf of steamy, soft bread in my arms. It was like a baby, a new baby, for us to have. The snow crunched under my feet, and I looked up to see my mother smiling down at me, her face pressed against the glass.

About the Author

Bushra Rehman grew up in Corona, Queens, but her mother says she was born in an ambulance flying through the streets of Brooklyn. Her father is not so sure. Since there are no definitive records of the time of her birth, there is no real way of knowing, but it would explain a few things. Bushra was a vagabond poet who traveled for years with nothing more than a Greyhound ticket and a book bag full of poems.

Bushra co-edited *Colonize This! Young Women of Color on Today's Feminism*. Rebecca Walker has called *Colonize This!* "a must for young women of color searching for themselves within contemporary feminist/womanist discourse and anyone else who wants to get down with the fierceness of fly, intellectual divas of color." *Colonize This!* was included in *Ms. Magazine*'s "100 Best Non-Fiction Books of All Time."

Bushra's poems, stories, and essays have been featured on BBC Radio 4, WNYC, and KPFA and in *The New York Times*, *India Currents*, *Crab Orchard Review*, *Sepia Mutiny*, *Color Lines*, *The Feminist Wire*, and *Mizna: Prose, Poetry and Art Exploring Arab America*. Bushra's poetry has been collected in the chapbook *Marianna's Beauty Salon*, and her writing has been anthologized in *Indivisible: Contemporary South Asian American Poetry*, *Collective Brightness: LGBTIQ Poets on Faith, Religion and Spirituality*, *And the World Changed: Contemporary Pakistani Women Writers*, and *Voices of Resistance: Muslim Women on War, Faith and Sexuality*.

Special thanks to those who helped make this book possible:

Sa'dia Rehman, Ben Perowsky, Andrea Dobrich, Anastacia Holt, Aisha Rehman, Chitra Ganesh, Rekha Malhotra, Yvette Ho, Sally Lee, Stas Gibbs, Diedra Barber, Saba Waheed, Adele Swank, Nina Sharma, Daisy Hernández, Bronwen Exter, Bryan Borland, Tara Sarath, Carroll Wallace, Chamindika Wanduragala, Claire and Derek Prime, Daniel Grushkin, Holly Blake, Ishle Yi Park, Jaishri Abichandani, Jeff Chang, Karen Russell, Marilyn Nelson, Michael Cunningham, Samantha Thornhill, Steve Zeitlin, Susan Choi, Asian American Writers' Workshop, Barbara Deming Memorial Foundation, Cave Canem, City Lore, Cullman Center for Teachers, Headlands Center for the Arts, Hedgebrook, Jerome Foundation, Kundiman, Norcroft, Saltonstall, Soul Mountain Retreat and the South Asian Women's Creative Collective.

About the Publisher

Sibling Rivalry Press is an independent publishing house based in Alexander, Arkansas. Learn more about Sibling Rivalry Press and download a Reader's Guide for this book at

www.siblingrivalrypress.com